Henry Charles Leonard

## Sacred Songs of the World

Translated from One Hundred and Twenty Languages

Henry Charles Leonard

**Sacred Songs of the World**
*Translated from One Hundred and Twenty Languages*

ISBN/EAN: 9783337181291

Printed in Europe, USA, Canada, Australia, Japan

Cover: Foto ©Andreas Hilbeck / pixelio.de

More available books at **www.hansebooks.com**

# SACRED SONGS OF THE WORLD.

Translated from
One Hundred and Twenty Languages.

EDITED BY

HENRY C. LEONARD, M.A.,

*Author of*

'*Sonnets on the Parables, and other Poems,*' '*John the Baptist: an
Epic Poem,*' '*Half-Hours with the Apostolic Fathers,*' '*A Literal
Translation of the Anglo-Saxon St. Mark,*' *etc.*

LONDON :
ELLIOT STOCK, 62, PATERNOSTER ROW, E.C.
1899.

To

THE RIGHT HONOURABLE

# PROFESSOR F. MAX MÜLLER,

A TEACHER OF TEACHERS

IN THE

KNOWLEDGE OF GOD AND MAN,

THIS ANTHOLOGY IS, BY PERMISSION,

GRATEFULLY INSCRIBED.

'Many shall come from the east and the west, and shall sit down with Abraham, and Isaac, and Jacob, in the Kingdom of Heaven.'—MATTHEW viii. 11.

'God is no respecter of persons, but in every nation he that feareth Him, and worketh righteousness, is acceptable to Him.'—ACTS x. 34.

'God made of one every nation of men to dwell on all the face of the earth, having determined their appointed seasons, and the bounds of their habitation; that they should seek God, if haply they might feel after Him, and find Him, though He is not far from each one of us, for in Him we live, and move, and have our being; as certain even of your own poets have said, "For we are also His offspring."'—ACTS xvii. 26 (Aratus, c. 5; Cleanthes, "Hymn to Jupiter").

'Wisdom reneweth all things, and, from generation to generation, passing into holy souls, she maketh men friends of God and Prophets.'—WISDOM vii. 27.

'A Prophet of their own.'—TITUS i. 12.

'He who is beloved of God honours every form of religious faith.'—GAUTAMA, THE BUDDHA.

# PREFACE.

FIFTY years ago, in the Preface to his ' Poetry and Poets of Europe,' the poet Longfellow wrote: ' Other languages I leave to some other hand, hoping that ere long a volume may be added to this which shall embrace all the remaining European tongues.' That Collection contained a large number of translations from ' the six Gothic languages of the North and the four Latin languages of the South.' Including a few representations of different stages of the same tongue, the following pages contain renderings from forty-eight European, thirty-nine Asiatic, twelve African, thirteen American and eight Oceanic languages.

The Collection is the fruit of many years' study of Comparative Theology and of the Poetry of civilized and uncivilized races, and has been prepared with the double purpose of promoting both these studies.

Previous sacred Anthologies have been gathered for Poetry's sake, or for the sake of some form of

Religion, orthodox or heterodox, or for both these objects combined. A somewhat different line is here followed. The piece representing each language is the best I could find in it for my purpose, but to exclude all which fail to reach a high poetic standard would defeat my object, by leaving important languages unrepresented. On the other hand, to exclude any form of Religious Thought, even the lower forms of Nature Worship (XXV., LXXV., LXXXVII.), would be inconsistent with the world-wide scope of the Collection. Where I have found, ready to hand, a translation by some standard author, such as Wordsworth (XXXI.), Shelley (XXV.), Longfellow (XVI., XVII., XXXVIII., etc.), or Bowring (XVIII., XX., XXI., etc.), I have been glad to use it. In many cases I have necessarily had to found on prose translations. To some of these I have given a simple metrical form, while others it seemed best to leave in their unadorned simplicity. Some of the latter, such as the Dirge from the Mangaian (CXV.), are of a very high order of poetic merit. In the translations for which I am myself responsible, I have aimed at great literalness. The longest piece in the book, Lamartine's Ode (XLVI.), which was circulated by tens of thousands at its first appearance, in 1830, and greatly admired for its poetic beauty and religious value, is here rendered in the varying metres of the original, and with corresponding rhymes. The Talmudic stories (LI., LIII.) have received a freer treatment.

In a few cases, such as the Cornish (XII.) and Manx (XIII.), the choice has been very limited indeed, while in some there is little or no written indigenous literature, as in Greenland (C.), where poetic utterances have been caught from the lips of natives by missionaries and travellers.

Poetry has, from the first, been the handmaid of Religion. According to Aristotle, it has 'a higher wisdom and a more serious worth than History.' It has been the permanent vehicle of great religious ideas, which have been handed down in it often more effectually than in creeds and articles of faith. ' Of the various modes of manifestation through which the human spirit pours its force,' says Matthew Arnold, 'that of the Poets is the most adequate and happy.' Hence it is in the Poetry of nations that we must look for the truest picture of their Religions.

Those who say that all Religions are alike speak ignorantly, yet it is the fact that the germs of truth may be found in all. 'The catholic-minded man,' says a Chinese sage, 'regards all religions as embodying the same truths ; the narrow-minded man observes only their differences.' In the theories of Theologians the differences are more apparent, in the songs of Poets the similarities. While creeds divide, hymns unite men, because sacred poetry gives the deepest utterance to those aspirations after the unseen and eternal which are common to all the human family.

Some of the most ancient religious Poetry is found to be the most pure, such as the lofty strains which reach us from the plains of Egypt (LXXXVIII.), or from the mountains of India (LXVIII.); while in a simple prayer from the iron-bound coasts of Patagonia (CXII.) may be found the great ideas of the Fatherhood of God, of His nearness to humanity, of Communion with Him. The 'light which lighteth every man' shone not only through Hebrew Prophets and Psalmists, but also through the constellation of great Teachers which blazoned out in the wonderful sixth century B.C.—Pythagoras, Confucius, Zoroaster and Buddha, nor through these alone, but through others not less great who are unknown to us by name, but whose words still echo through the world.

Instructive parallels may be found by the student of comparative Religion. As in the history of Israel we see Religion suffering long in the hands of priests, reviving through the ministry of Poet-prophets, so in later times 'prophets of their own' have appeared in Asia, such as Vemana (LXXI.) and Nanuk (LXXIII.), and in America, such as the Royal Psalmist of undiscovered Mexico, Nezahualcoyotl (CVII.). On the other hand, we may mark the wide-spread tendency to pay divine honours to those who would themselves have earnestly repudiated them, as in the case of Buddha (LXXXIII.), the Mother of Christ (LXIV.), the son-in-law of Mohammed (LXVII.), much as afterwards Englishmen prayed to St. Thomas of Canterbury, and Frenchmen to St. Denys, as often as to their Creator.

' Nothing to my mind,' says Professor Max-Müller, ' can be sadder than reading the sacred books of mankind, and yet nothing more encouraging.  They are full of rubbish ; but among that rubbish there are old stones which the builders of the true Temple of Humanity will not reject—must not reject, if their Temple is to hold all who worship God in spirit and in truth.'

I gratefully acknowledge my obligation to the Right Honourable Professor Max-Müller for much help derived from the study of his works, for the use of his rendering of a Vedic Hymn and of Buddha's ' Triumph Song ' revised to the present date, and for permission to inscribe my book to him ; to the late Right Honourable W. E. Gladstone for access to St. Deiniol's Library, Hawarden (generously thrown open for the use of all students), where I have found help not easily attainable elsewhere ; to the Rev. Dr. Pope, of the Indian Institute, Oxford, for his literal rendering of Vacagar's hymn from the Tamil; to Professor Mackinnon, of Edinburgh, and the Rev. Dr. Norman Macleod for enabling me to find the late Dr. Nicholson's beautiful rendering of St. Columba's Hymn, translated from the MS. in the Royal Library, Brussels, and to Miss Nicholson for permitting its use ; to Mr. H. A. Giles, of Aberdeen, formerly H.M.'s Vice-Consul at Shanghai, for the use of his translation from the Chinese poet Su Tung-P'o ;

to Messrs. Macmillan for that of the late Professor Blackie's translation from Modern Greek; to the Rev. A. Sowerby, of Shansi, China, for a hymn from Modern Chinese; to the Rev. T. Haines, of Belgaum, India, for one from the Canarese; and to the Rev. A. L. Jenkins, of Morlaix, Britanny, for the use of one of his hymns written in the Breton language, and for his aid in the translation of it.

Many names and many Religions are honoured in these pages, but chiefly the ' Name which is above every name,' and the Religion which, unlike the decaying Religions around it, is making its way with ever-increasing energy and success in the four quarters of the world.

> ' A power from the unknown God,
>   A Promethean conqueror came ;
> Like a triumphal path, he trod
>   The thorns of death and shame.
>     A mortal shape to him
>     Was like the vapour dim
> Which the orient planet animates with light ;
>     Hell, Sin and Slavery came,
>     Like bloodhounds mild and tame,
> Nor preyed until their lord had taken flight.
>     The moon of Mahomet
>     Arose,—and it shall set !
> While, blazoned, as on heaven's immortal noon,
>   The Cross leads generations on." (SHELLEY.)

10, GORDON ROAD,     H. C. LEONARD.
CLIFTON.

*Note.*—This book is printed from the manuscript completed shortly before the editor's death. It has not had the advantage of his revision in proof, hence one or two trifling omissions.

# CONTENTS.

## EUROPE.

## EUROPE—*continued.*

## EUROPE—*continued.*

## ASIA—*continued.*

## AFRICA.

## AFRICA—*continued.*

## AMERICA.

## AMERICA—*continued.*

## OCEANIA.

# EUROPE.

# BRITAIN.

*FROM THE ANGLO-SAXON OF CAEDMON.*

## I.—THE CREATION.

In the beginning, first, the eternal Lord,
Head of all creatures, shaped the heaven and earth,
The firmament upreared, this roomy land
Established by His power, almighty King !
Nor was the field yet green with springing grass,
For, far and wide, swart in eternal night,
The ocean covered o'er the darksome ways.
Then, o'er the deep, the glorious Spirit of Him
Who guards the heaven was borne with mighty speed,
And the Life-giver, He who made the angels,
Bade light come forth over the roomy deep.
Then quickly was fulfilled the great King's word,
And, o'er the waste, the holy light shone out,
E'en as the Maker bade.   Then, o'er the flood,
The Lord of Triumphs sundered dark from light,
Brightness from shadows.   The Life-giver next
Gave names to both : and, first, the holy light,
By the Lord's word, received the name of Day.
Creation beauty-bright !   Well pleased was then

[ 3 ]                     1—2

The Lord at the beginning,—teeming time!
The first day saw the gloomy shadow dark
Prevailing, swart, beyond the wide abyss.
Then passed the time above the fruitless waste
Of middle earth.   The Maker next put forth,—
Our great Creator,—from the brightness sheer
The evening first, and in its footsteps soon
Pressed on apace the misty cloud on which
The Lord Himself bestowed the name of Night.
He who preserves our life did sunder them:
And, always since, these two, in all the earth,
Ever have borne and done their Maker's will.

　Then came the second day, light after dark,
Now bade Life's Guardian, on the flood of mere,
The joyful heaven-frame in the midst uprise.
Our Ruler dealt the waters, and then wrought
The steadfast firmament: this the Mighty hove
Up from the earth, by His all-powerful word.
The earth beneath the lofty firmament
Was, by His holy might, divided off
Water from waters, for those dwelling yet
Under the firmness of the nation's roof.

　Then came, o'er all the earth, quick journeying,
The third great morn.   Nor was there meted yet
The widespread land, nor traced the useful ways.
The earth stood covered fast with swelling flood.
Then, by His word, the Lord of angels bade
The open waters be, that hold their course
Beneath the firmament with places fixed.
Then quickly stood beneath the arching heaven
The ocean,—as the Holy One decreed,
Wide-gathered.   Thus the water from the land

Was sundered.   Then the Guardian of our life,
Preserver of all good, saw, wide displayed,
The places dry, and these the Glory-King
Named Earth, and to the roomy flood of waves
Prescribed their rightful course.

*      *      *      *      *

Then to the Guardian of the firmament
It seemed not fit Adam should longer stay
Alone the keeper of the Field of Rest,
Sole tenant of the new-created world.
For him the King most high, the almighty Lord,
A helper therefore made, a wife upraised.
Her, for a prop to the beloved man,
The Author of the light of life bestowed.
The substance took from Adam's body out,
And skilfully a rib removed away
From out the side ; and motionless was he
And softly slept, nor knew he any sore,
Nor share of pain, nor came there any blood
From out the wound !   For him the angels' Lord
Out of his body took a jointed bone,—
The man unwounded,—and of that God wrought
A noble maiden, and within her frame
Created life, and an immortal soul.
Like angels were they !   Then was Adam's bride
With spirit filled ; and both, in prime of youth,
Were bright with beauty, in the world brought forth
By the Creator's might ; nor knew they sin
To do nor suffer from, but burning love
Was theirs, in both their breasts, unto the Lord.

H. C. LEONARD.

# BRITAIN.

*FROM THE ANGLO-NORMAN, OR SEMI-SAXON* (A.D. 1150).

## II.—THE GRAVE.

FOR thee a house was made
   Ere thou wast born ;
For thee a mould was laid
   Ere thy birth-morn.
It is not yet prepared,
   Nor is its depth decreed,
Nor is it yet declared
   What length of wall thou'lt need.
Now will I make thee see
   Where thou shalt soon be found ;
Now will I measure thee,
   And, after that, the ground !

The house for thy behoof
   No ceiling high doth own ;
Not far is raised the roof
   O'er its foundation stone ;
The threshold is but low,
   The passages depressed,
The roof is timbered—so
   As just to clear thy breast !

[ 6 ]

So shalt thou, in the mould,
  In gloomy darkness be,
And, in thy chamber cold,
  Lie long and lonesomely.

No door that house doth own
  Where thou shalt prisoned be ;
No window there is known,
  And Death doth hold the key.
Full loathsome is that cell,
  And grim wherein to stay,
Yet in it thou shalt dwell,
  And worms shall on thee prey.

When this shall be thy home,
  From all thy loved ones rent,
No friend to thee shall come
  To see if thou'rt content ;
And none shall pass its portal
  Intent to set thee free,
For what of thee is mortal
  Shall naught but loathsome be.

H. C. LEONARD.

*FROM THE MIDDLE ENGLISH OF CHAUCER* (A.D. 1388).

### III.—THE GOOD PARSON.

THE parson of a country town was he,
Who knew the straits of humble poverty ;
But rich he was in holy thought and work,
Nor less in learning, as became a clerk.
The word of Christ most truly did he preach.
And his parishioners devoutly teach.
Benign was he, in labours diligent,
And in adversity was still content—
As proved full oft.    To all his flock a friend,
Averse was he to ban or to contend
When tithes were due.    Much rather was he found,
Unto his poor parishioners around,
Of his own substance and his dues to give,
Content on little, for himself, to live.
　　Wide was his parish, scattered far asunder.
Yet none did he neglect, in rain or thunder.
Sorrow and sickness won his kindly care ;
With staff in hand he travelled everywhere.
This good example to his sheep he brought
That first he wrought, and afterwards he taught.

## THE GOOD PARSON

This parable he joined the Word unto—
That, ' If gold rust what shall the iron do ?'
For if a priest be foul, in whom we trust,
No wonder if a common man should rust !
And shame it were, in those the flock who keep,
For shepherds to be foul, yet clean the sheep.
Well ought a priest example fair to give,
By his own cleanness, how his sheep should live.
    He did not put his benefice to hire,
And leave his sheep encumbered in the mire,
Then hasten to St. Paul's, in London town,
To seek a chantry where to settle down,
And there at ease to sing the daily mass,
Or with a Brotherhood his time to pass.
He dwelt at home, with watchful care to keep
From prowling wolves his well-protected sheep.
    Though holy in himself and virtuous,
He still to sinful men was piteous.
Not sparing of his speech, in vain conceit,
But in his teaching kindly and discreet.
To draw his flock to Heaven with noble art,
By good example, was his holy part.
Nor less did he rebuke the obstinate,
Whether they were of high or low estate.
For pomp and worldly show he did not care,
No morbid conscience made his rule severe.
The lore of Christ and His apostles twelve
He taught, but first he followed it himself.

H. C. Leonard.

# BRITAIN.

*FROM THE ENGLISH OF ALEXANDER POPE* (A.D. 1738).

## IV.—A UNIVERSAL PRAYER.

FATHER of all ! in every age,
   In every clime adored
By saint, by savage, and by sage,
   Jehovah, Jove, or Lord !

Thou great First Cause, least understood,
   Who all my sense confined
To know but this, that Thou art good,
   And that myself am blind ;

Yet gave me, in this dark estate,
   To see the good from ill ;
And, binding nature fast in fate,
   Left free the human will.

What conscience dictates to be done,
   Or warns me not to do,
This, teach me more than hell to shun,
   That, more than heaven pursue.

[ 10 ]

What blessings Thy free bounty gives
 Let me not cast away ;
For God is paid when man receives ;
 To enjoy is to obey.

Yet not to earth's contracted span
 Thy goodness let me bound,
Or think Thee Lord alone of man,
 When thousand worlds are round.

Let not this weak, unknowing hand
 Presume Thy bolts to throw,
And deal damnation round the land
 On each I judge Thy foe.

If I am right, Thy grace impart
 Still in the right to stay ;
If I am wrong, O teach my heart
 To find that better way !

Save me alike from foolish pride,
 Or impious discontent,
At aught Thy wisdom has denied,
 Or aught Thy goodness lent.

Teach me to feel another's woe,
 To hide the fault I see ;
That mercy l to others show,
 That mercy show to me.

Mean though I am, not wholly so
 Since quickened by Thy breath ;
O lead me, wheresoe'er I go,
 Through this day's life, or death !

This day, be bread and peace my lot ;
  All else beneath the sun
Thou know'st if best bestowed or not,
  And let Thy will be done.

To Thee, whose temple is all space,
  Whose altar, earth, sea, skies !
One chorus let all being raise !
  All Nature's incense rise !

# BRITAIN.

*FROM THE OLD LOWLAND SCOTTISH OF W. DUNBAR*
(A.D. 1507).

## V.—Pious Mirth.

Be merry, man, nor keep too sore in mind
   The wavering of this wretched world of sorrow;
To God be humble, to thy friend be kind,
   And with thy neighbour gladly lend and borrow;
   His fate to-night, it may be thine to-morrow;
Be glad at heart whate'er thy lot on earth,
   For true this word of wisdom thou wilt find—
Wealth without gladness is of little worth.


Make thee good cheer with all that God may send,
   For without welfare worldly luck is naught;
No good is thine except what thou dost spend,
   The rest is e'er with constant sorrow fraught;
   When sorrow comes let solace then be sought;
Thy life may not endure bereft of mirth,
   Wherefore with comfort let thy footsteps wend;
Wealth without gladness is of little worth.

Be pitiful, flee trouble and debate,
  With people of good fame keep company ;
Kindly and humble be in thine estate,
  For worldly honour lasts but for a cry.
  In earthly trouble be not melancholy ;
Be rich in patience, e'en in time of dearth ;
  For he who merry lives lives mightily ;
Wealth without gladness is of little worth.

Thou seest poor wretches filled with grief and care
  To heap up treasure till their days shall end ;
And when their bags are full their souls are bare !
  To keep their riches all their powers they bend.
  While others with less grace have them to spend
Who in the winning had no part on earth !
  Example take ! and gladly spend thy share ;
Wealth without gladness is of little worth.

Though all the toil that e'er had living wight
  Were thine alone, no more to thee doth fall
Than meat and clothes, and of the rest a sight !
  Yet to the Judge thou'lt give account of all.
  Right reckonings happen when the bill is small.
Be just, wrong none, maintain a cheerful mirth,
  And truth shall make thee strong as any wall ;
Wealth without gladness is of little worth.

                              H. C. LEONARD.

# BRITAIN.

*FROM THE SCOTTISH GAELIC OF ST. COLUMBA.*

## VI.—St. Columba's Hymn.

'Tis sweet, by the Scottish main,
  On a rocky crag to rest,
And to gaze, again and again,
  On the ocean's boundless breast.

To look on the waves as they swell,
  While they chant in their Father's ear
Their melodies sweet, and tell
  Of the course of the world's career.

To gaze at the starlit shore,
  With its smooth and level strand,
And to hear the birds, as they soar
  And sail, o'er sea and land.

The thunder of crowding waves
  To hear on the rocky shore,
And, down where the water laves
  The cliff, by the church's door.

To watch the flocks, whose wings
   Sweep o'er the watery plain,
And—greatest of wonderful things—
   The monsters of the main.

To see the ebb and the flow
   In power upon the sea,
When ' Farewell to Erin,' I know,
   My secret name must be !

Then grief my heart would fill,
   While gazing towards Erin's shore,
And all that I've done of ill
   I, weeping, would deplore.

To God would I give my thanks—
   Him who doth all things keep—
Heaven with its serried ranks,
   And earth, and shore, and deep.

I would search in all the lore
   That good to my soul might bring ;
Now Heaven I would adore,
   And now a psalm I'd sing.

Heaven's high One, the King of Saints,
   My thoughts would now employ ;
And to work without constraints
   Would fill my heart with joy.

Sweet weeds from the rocks I'd pick ;
   At times I'd fishing go ;
Anon I would tend the sick,
   And now in the cell bend low.

Best counsel unto me
  My gracious God hath given ;
From error He'll keep me free
  My King, the Lord of Heaven !

A. Nicolson.
H. C. Leonard.

# BRITAIN.

*FROM THE IRISH GAELIC OF ST. PATRICK* (A.D. 433).

## VII.—St. Patrick's Hymn.

CHRIST as a light
Illumine and guide me!
Christ as a shield o'ershadow and cover me!
Christ be beside me,
On left hand and right hand!
Christ be before me, behind me, about me!
Christ the lowly and the meek,
Christ the All-powerful, be
In the heart of each to whom I speak,
In the mouth of each who speaks to me,
In all who draw near me,
Or see me, or hear me!

J. C. MANGAN.

# BRITAIN.

*FROM THE MODERN IRISH GAELIC OF MAC AN BHAIRD.*

## VIII.—Mourners Comforted.

O Mourner of thy lost ones, dry
   Thine overflowing eyes, and turn
     Thine heart aside;
For Adam's race is born to die,
   And sternly the sepulchral urn
     Mocks human pride!

Look not, nor sigh, for earthly throne,
   Nor place thy trust in arm of clay,
     But, on thy knees,
Uplift thy soul to God alone,
   For all things go their destined way
     As He decrees.

Embrace the faithful Crucifix,
   And seek the path of pain and prayer
     Thy Saviour trod!
Nor let thy spirit intermix
   With earthly hope and worldly care
     Its groans to God!

        2—2

And Thou, O mighty Lord ! whose ways
   Are far above our feeble minds
     To understand,
Sustain us in these doleful days,
   And render light the chain that binds
     Our fallen land !

Look down upon our dreary state,
   And through the ages that may still
     Roll on apace,
Watch Thou o'er Erin's hapless fate,
   And shield at least from darker ill
     Her suffering race.

               J. C. MANGAN.

# BRITAIN.

*FROM THE OLD WELSH OF TALHAIARN* (A.D. 550).

## IX.—TALHAIARN'S PRAYER.

GRANT me, O God, Thy merciful protection ;
And, in protection, give me strength, I pray ;
And, in my strength, O grant me wise discretion ;
And, in discretion, make me ever just ;
And, with my justice, may I mingle love ;
And, with my love, O God, the love of Thee ;
And, with the love of Thee, the love of all.

SHARON TURNER.

# BRITAIN.

*FROM THE MIDDLE WELSH OF MADAWG AB GUALLTER*
(A.D. 1250).

## X.—PRAISE ON A HARP.

JESUS, fair Jesus, let me see Thy face !
   O turn it not away,
Nor veil Thy features.   Look on me in grace,
   And hate me not, I pray.

Mysterious Ruler, give me stronger faith.
   O take my hand in Thine,
And guide my wandering steps through life and death,
   In rectitude's straight line.

Each one who knows Thee, Ruler of the days,
   His joyful music brings,
With bells and tuneful harps to sound Thy praise
   From sharp and twanging strings.

When Heaven and Earth and Hell are at Thy bar
   O mark me with Thy Name !
To count me with the damned Thou wouldst not care,
   Then place me by the Lamb.

[ 22 ]

So, in the day of trouble and of ire,
  Let me before Thee stand
Among the happy, faultless, white-robed choir,
  Ever at Thy right hand.

                    T. STEPHENS.
                    H. C. LEONARD.

# BRITAIN.

*FROM THE MODERN WELSH OF W. WILLIAMS* (1772).

## XI.—The Pilgrimage of Life.

Guide me, O Thou great Jehovah,
  Pilgrim through this barren land;
I am weak, but Thou art mighty;
  Hold me with Thy powerful hand.
    Bread of heaven,
Feed me, till I want no more.

Open Thou the crystal fountain
  Whence the healing streams do flow;
Let the fiery, cloudy pillar
  Lead me all my journey through;
    Strong Deliverer,
Be Thou still my strength and shield.

When I tread the verge of Jordan,
  Bid my anxious fears subside;
Death of Death, and Hell's destruction,
  Land me safe on Canaan's side;
    Songs of praises
I will ever give to Thee.

W. Evans.

[ 24 ]

# BRITAIN.

*FROM THE CORNISH.*

## XII.—From a Passion Play.

Hear, O good people, all the tale we tell !
Now have you seen set forth how Jesus died
A martyr's death, for love of all the world.
May Jesus, full of grace, bless one and all !

Now go.   Reflect upon His passion sore
Each in his heart, and let each heart be true !
Not for Himself He suffered certainly ;
It was for love of all the sons of men.

O show thy love to Him !   By day and night,
With all thy heart, Him worship and adore !
When from thy home on earth thou pass away
Then shalt thou dwell for ever in His court.

May Jesus, full of grace, bless one and all !
Now hasten homeward, for the Play is done,
And come, when morning dawns, that all may see
How from the tomb Christ rose, gentle and bright.

E. Morris.<br>
H. C. Leonard.

[ 25 ]

# BRITAIN.

*FROM THE MANX OF S. RUTTER* (A.D. 1645)

## XIII.—THE SOUL'S ANCHOR.

My mind with troubles vext, my heart with grief annoyed,
My head with cares perplext, my all of comfort void,
Upon this stony pillow I seek my rest in vain,
And, just like yonder billow, my thoughts do swell again.

These rocks below are shaken and torn as well as I,
Our strength is all mistaken, and we are found a lie,
The waves, with often beating, have eaten into stone,
Whilst ills, with oft repeating, have made my heart to
groan.

When by a storm are clustered the waters of the sky
And all to ruin mustered but this poor rock and I,
And ships, like shells, are sinking for all their oaken sides,
O then shall I be thinking of all deceitful tides.

And thus my harms recounting, upon this cliff I rest,
My ship no longer mounting, my anchor in my breast,
Which, when it came in hither, methought I heard one say,
' We shall have change of weather, and see a fairer day.'

S. RUTTER (*Trans.*).

[ 26 ]

# ICELAND.

*FROM THE ICELANDIC OR NORSE* (A.D. 750).

## XIV.—VOLA'S PROPHECY.

THE sun turns pale!
The sea engulfs
The spacious earth!
From heaven fall
The lustrous stars,
At end of time!
The vapours rage;
And darting flames
Involve the skies!


She sees arise,
The second time,
From the sea, the earth,
Completely green!
Cascades descend;
The eagle soars,
And, on the hills,
Pursues his prey!

[ 27 ]

The gods convene
On Ida's plains,
And talk of man,
The worm of dust.
They call to mind
Their former might,
And the ancient runes
Of Fimbultyr.

The fields, unsown,
Shall yield their crop!
All ills shall cease!
Balder shall come
And dwell with Hauthr
In Hroft's abodes!
Say, warrior gods,
Conceive ye yet?

A hall she sees
Outshine the sun!
Of gold the roof!
It stands in heaven!
The virtuous there
Shall always dwell,
And evermore
Delights enjoy!

HENDERSON.

# NORWAY.

*FROM THE NORWEGIAN OF B. BJÖRNSON.*

## XV.—THE WINGS OF A DOVE.

WHAT shall I see, if I ever go
  Over the mountains high ?
Now I can see but the peaks of snow,
Crowning the cliffs where the pine-trees grow,
  Waiting, and longing to rise,
  Nearing the beckoning skies.

The eagle is rising afar away
  Over the mountains high,
Rowing along in the radiant day,
With mighty strokes, to his distant prey,
  Swooping, where he will, downwards,
  Sailing, where he will, onwards.

Apple-tree, longest thou not to go
  Over the mountains high ?
Gladly thou growest in summer's glow,
Patiently waitest through winter's snow ;
  Though birds on thy branches swing,
  Thou knowest not what they sing.

[ 29 ]

Birds, with your chattering, why did ye come
    Over the mountains high ?
Beyond, in a summer land, ye could roam,
And nearer to heaven could build your home :
    Why have ye come to bring
    Longing, without your wing ?

Shall I then never, never flee
    Over the mountains high ?
Rocky walls, will ye always be
Prisons until ye are tombs for me ?
    Until I lie at your feet
    Wrapped in my winding sheet ?

Away ! away !   I will soar away
    Over the mountains high !
Here, I am sinking lower each day,
Though my spirit has chosen the loftiest way ;
    Let her in freedom fly,
    Not beat on the walls and die !

*Once* I know I shall journey far
    Over the mountains high !
Lord, is Thy door already ajar ?
Dear is the home where Thy saved ones are :
    But bar it awhile from me,
    And help me to long for Thee !

S. Rugeley-Powers.

# SWEDEN.

*FROM THE SWEDISH OF BISHOP TEGNER.*

## XVI.—ASPIRATION.

SON of Eternity, fettered in time, and an exile, the spirit
Tugs at his chains evermore, and struggles, like flame, ever
    upward.
Still he recalls, with emotion, his Father's manifold
    mansions,
Thinks of the land of his fathers, where blossomed more
    freshly the flowerets,
Shone a more beautiful sun, and he played with the wìngèd
    angels.
Then grows the earth too narrow, too close ; and, homesick
    for heaven,
Longs the wanderer again ; and the spirit's longings are
    worship !
Worship is called his most beautiful hour, and its tongue
    is entreaty.
Ah ! when the infinite burden of life descendeth upon us,
Crushes to earth our hope, and, under the earth, in the
    graveyard,
Then it is good to pray unto God ; for His sorrowing
    children

Turns he ne'er from His door, but He heals and helps and
    consoles them.
Yet it is better to pray when all things are fortunate
    with us—
Pray in fortunate days ; for life's most beautiful Fortune
Kneels before the Eternal's throne, and, with hands inter-
    folded,
Praises, thankful and moved, the only Giver of blessings.

H. W. LONGFELLOW.

# DENMARK.

*FROM THE DANISH OF BAGGESEN.*

## XVII.—MEMORIES OF CHILDHOOD.

THERE was a time when I was very small,
    When my whole frame was but an ell in height,
Sweetly, as I recall it, tears do fall,
    And therefore I recall it with delight.

Then seemed to me the world far less in size,
    Likewise it seemed to me less wicked far ;
Like points in heaven, I saw the stars arise,
    And longed for wings that I might catch a star.

I saw the moon behind the island fade,
    And thought, ' O, were I on that island there
I could find out of what the moon is made,
    Find out how large it is, how round, how fair !'

Wondering, I saw God's sun, through western skies,
    Sink in the ocean's golden lap at night,
And yet upon the morrow early rise,
    And paint the eastern heaven with crimson light ;

And thought of God, the gracious Heavenly Father
　Who made me, and that lovely sun on high,
And all those pearls of heaven thick-strung together
　Dropped, clustering, from His hand o'er all the sky.

With childish reverence, my young lips did say
　The prayer my pious mother taught to me :
' O gentle God !   O let me strive alway
　Still to be wise and good, and follow Thee !'

So prayed I for my father and my mother,
　And for my sister, and for all the town ;
The king I knew not, nor the beggar-brother
　Who, bent with age, went sighing up and down.

They perished, the blithe days of childhood perished,
　And all the gladness, all the peace I knew !
Now have I but their memory, fondly cherished—
　God ! may I never, never lose that too !

H. W. Longfellow.

# HOLLAND.

*FROM THE DUTCH OF VAN VONDEL.*

## XVIII.—ADAM'S HYMN IN PARADISE.

O FATHER, we approach Thy throne,
  Who bidst the glorious sun arise,
  All-good, Almighty, and All-wise,
Great source of all things, God alone !

We see Thee !  Brighter than the rays
  Of the bright sun, we see Thee shine !
  As in a fountain's face, divine,
We see Thee, endless Fount of days !

We see Thee, who our frames hast wrought,
  With one swift word, from senseless clay ;
  Waked, with one glance of heavenly ray,
Our never-dying souls from naught !

Those souls Thou lightedst with the spark
  At Thy pure fire ; and, gracious still,
  Gav'st immortality, free-will,
And language not involved or dark !

SIR J. BOWRING.

# HOLLAND.

*FROM THE MODERN FRISIAN* (A.D. 1834).

## XIX.—LIFE AND DEATH.

WHAT art thou, Life ?
A weary strife
   Of pain, and need, and sorrow ;
Long hours of grief
And joys how brief
   That vanish on the morrow.

Death, what art thou ?
To whom all bow,
   From sceptred king to slave ;
The last best friend
Our cares to end,
   Thy empire is the grave.

BOSWORTH.

# RUSSIA.

*FROM THE RUSS OF GABRIEL ROMANOVITCH DERZ-HAVIN* (A.D. 1793).

## XX.—GOD.

O THOU Eternal One ! whose presence bright
   All space doth occupy, all motion guide ;
Unchanged through time's all-devastating flight ;
   Thou only God ! There is no God beside !
Being above all beings ! Mighty One !
   Whom none can comprehend, and none explore ;
Who fill'st existence with Thyself alone :
   Embracing all, supporting, ruling o'er,
   Being whom we call God, and know no more !

In its sublime research, philosophy
   May measure out the ocean-deep, may count
The sands, or the sun's rays, but God ! for Thee
   There is no weight nor measure ; none can mount
Up to Thy mysteries ; Reason's brightest spark,
   Though kindled by Thy light, in vain would try
To trace Thy counsels, infinite and dark :
   And thought is lost ere thought can soar so high,
   E'en like past moments in eternity.

[ 37 ]

Thou from primeval nothingness didst call
    First chaos, then existence ; Lord ! on Thee
Eternity had its foundation : all
    Sprung forth from Thee : of light, joy, harmony
Sole origin ; all life, all beauty Thine !
    Thy word created all, and doth create ;
Thy splendour fills all space with rays divine.
    Thou art, and wert, and shalt be ! Glorious ! Great !
    Light-giving, life-sustaining Potentate !


Thy chains the unmeasured universe surround :
    Upheld by Thee, by Thee inspired with breath.
Thou the beginning with the end hath bound,
    And beautifully mingled life and death.        .
As sparks mount upwards from the fiery blaze
    So suns are born, so worlds spring forth from Thee ;
And as the spangles in the sunny rays
    Shine round the silver snow, the pageantry
    Of heaven's bright army glitters in Thy praise.


A million torches lighted by Thy hand
    Wander unwearied through the blue abyss ;
They own Thy power, accomplish Thy command,
    All gay with life, all eloquent with bliss.
What shall we call them ?   Piles of crystal light ?
    A glorious company of golden streams ?
Lamps of celestial ether burning bright ?
    Suns lighting systems with their glorious beams ?
    But Thou to these art as the noon to night.

Yes ! as a drop of water in the sea,
   All this magnificence in Thee is lost !
What are ten thousand worlds compared to Thee ?
   And what am I, then ?   Heaven's unnumbered host
Though multiplied by myriads, and arrayed
   In all the glory of sublimest thought,
Is but an atom in the balance weighed
   Against Thy greatness ; is a cypher brought
   Against infinity.   What am I then ?   Naught !


Naught ?   But the effluence of Thy light divine,
   Pervading worlds, hath reached my bosom too ;
Yes ! in my spirit doth Thy spirit shine
   As shines the sunbeam in a drop of dew.
Naught !   But I live, and on hope's pinions fly
   Eager to reach Thy presence ; for in Thee
I live, and breathe, and dwell ; aspiring high,
   E'en to the throne of Thy divinity.
   I am, O God ! and surely Thou must be !


Thou art ! directing, guiding all, Thou art !
   Direct my understanding then to Thee ;
Control my spirit, guide my wandering heart ;
   Though but an atom midst immensity
Still I am something !   Fashioned by Thy hand
   I hold a middle rank 'twixt heaven and earth,
On the last verge of mortal being stand,
   Close to the realms where angels have their birth,
   Just on the boundaries of the spirit-land !

The chain of being is complete in me,
    In me is matter's last gradation lost ;
And the next step is spirit, Deity !
    I can command the lightning, and am dust !
A monarch, and a slave !   A worm, a god !
    Whence came I here, and how so wondrously
Constructed and conceived ? unknown ! this clod
    Lives surely through some higher energy,
    For from itself alone it could not be.


Creator, yes ! Thy wisdom and Thy word
    Created *me /*   Thou source of life and good !
Thou spirit of my spirit, and my Lord !
    Thy light, Thy love, in their bright plenitude
Filled an immortal soul, destined to spring
    O'er the abyss of death, and bade it wear
The garments of eternal day, and wing
    Its heavenly flight beyond this little sphere,
    E'en to its source, to Thee, its author there.


O thoughts ineffable !   O visions blest !
    Though worthless our conceptions all of Thee,
Yet shall Thy shadowed image fill our breast,
    And waft its homage to Thy Deity.
God ! thus alone my lowly thoughts can soar ;
    Thus seek Thy presence, Being wise and good !
Midst Thy vast works admire, obey, adore ;
    And, when the tongue is eloquent no more,
    The soul shall speak in tears of gratitude.

SIR J. BOWRING.

# RUSSIA.

*FROM THE SCLAVONIC OF BOBROV.*

## XXI.—THE GOLDEN PALACE.

THE golden palace of my God
  Towering above the clouds I see,
Beyond the cherubs' bright abode,
  Higher than angels' thoughts can be ;
How can I in those courts appear
  Without a wedding garment on ?
Conduct me, Thou life-giver, there,
  Conduct me to Thy glorious throne !
And clothe me with Thy robes of light,
And lead me through sin's darksome night,
  My Saviour and my God !

SIR J. BOWRING.

# RUSSIA.

*FROM THE FINNISH.*

## XXII.—Jumala's Chariot.

Harness now Thyself, Jumala,
Ruler of the air, Thy horses !
Bring them forth, Thy rapid racers,
Drive the sledge with glittering colours,
Passing through our bones, our ankles,
Through our flesh, that shakes and trembles,
Through our veins, which seem all broken !
Knit the flesh and bones together,
Fasten vein to vein more firmly.
Let our joints be filled with silver,
Let our veins with gold be running !

Castren.
F. Max-Müller.

# TURKEY-IN-EUROPE.

*FROM THE OUIGOUR—ANCIENT TURKISH* (A.D. 750).

## XXIII.—GOD AND HIS PROPHET.

LET praise be rendered unto God Most High,
The King of Power, of glory infinite :
Creator of the earth and of the sky,
Who to each body doth a soul unite ;
Who all performs as His great will decrees ;
Who everything ordains as He doth please !
The peace of God, and blessing without end,
Upon the Wonder of all Time descend !
The Best of Messengers who earth hath trod,
Mohammed, Prophet of the Most High God !

A. L. DAVIDS.
H. C. LEONARD.

# TURKEY-IN-EUROPE.

*FROM THE MODERN TURKISH OF FAZEL* (A.D. 1550).

## XXIV.—AN ELEGY ON A PRINCESS.

ALAS ! thou laidst her low, malicious Death,
    Enjoyment's pleasant cup yet half unquaffed !
The hour-glass out, thou'st robbed her of her breath,
    While, joyful, in life's budding spring, she laughed.

This fair white pearl, a prince, with kingdom wide,
    Counted his soul's best treasure, and his pride ;
O earth !   All fondly cradle her to rest !
    O welcome her with smiles, thou Seraph blest !

ANON.

H. C. LEONARD.

# GREECE.

*FROM THE GREEK OF HOMER.*

## XXV.—HYMN TO THE EARTH.

O UNIVERSAL Mother, who dost keep,
From everlasting, thy foundations deep,
Eldest of things, Great Earth, I sing of thee !
All shapes that have their dwelling in the sea,
All things that fly, or on the ground divine
Live, move, and there are nourished, these are thine ;
These from thy wealth thou dost sustain ; from thee
Fair babes are born ; and fruits on every tree
Hang ripe and large, revered Divinity !
   The life of mortal men beneath thy sway
Is held ; thy power both gives and takes away !
Happy are they whom thy mild favours nourish,
All things unstinted round them grow and flourish.
For them endures the life-sustaining field
Its load of harvest, and their cattle yield
Large increase, and their house with wealth is filled.
Such honoured dwell in cities fair and free,
The homes of lovely women, prosperously ;
Their sons exult in youth's new-budding gladness,
And their fresh daughters, free from care or sadness,

With bloom-inwoven dance and happy song,
On the soft flowers the meadow-grass among,
Leap around them sporting !   Such delights by thee
Are given, rich Power, revered Divinity !
    Mother of gods, thou wife of starry Heaven,
Farewell !   Be thou propitious, and be given
A happy life for this brief melody,
Nor thou, nor other songs, shall unremembered be.

SHELLEY.

# GREECE.

*FROM THE MEDIAEVAL GREEK OF ST. JOSEPH OF THE STUDIUM* (A.D. 850).

## XXVI.—THE FINISHED COURSE.

SAFE home, safe home in port ; ·
  Strained cordage, shattered deck,
Torn sails, provisions short,
  And only not a wreck ;
But O the joy, upon the shore,
To tell our voyage perils o'er !

The prize, the prize secure !
  The wrestler nearly fell ;
Bore all he could endure,
  And bore not always well ;
But he may smile at troubles gone
Who sets the victor's garland on.

No more the foe can harm ;
  No more of leaguered camp,
And cry of night-alarm,
  And need of ready lamp ;

And yet how nearly he had failed !
How nearly had the foe prevailed !

The lamb is in the fold,
   In perfect safety penned ;
The lion once had hold,
   And thought to make an end ;
But One came by with wounded side,
And, for the sheep, the Shepherd died.

The exile is at home ;
   O nights and days of tears !
O longings not to roam !
   O sins, and doubts, and fears !
What matters now ?   O joyful day !
The King hath wiped all tears away.

O happy, happy bride,
   The widowed hours are past !
The Bridegroom at thy side,
   Thou all His own at last ;
The sorrows of thy former cup
In full fruition swallowed up.

                     J. M. NEALE.

# GREECE.

*FROM THE MODERN GREEK.*

## XXVII.—The March of Death.

' Why are the hills so dusky red ?
  So dark and sable-shrouded ?
Is it the wind, on the craggy head,
  Is it the sky that's clouded ?'
'Tis not the wind on the craggy head,
  'Tis not the rain that's beating ;
'Tis only Death with his troop of dead
  That o'er the hills is fleeting !

The young he drives his path before ;
  The old he drags behind him ;
The tender babes, though weeping sore,
  Fast on his saddle binding.
The old beseech the rider grim,
  The young with tears down-flowing,
' O tarry, Death, by the cottage trim,
  Where the fountain cool is glowing.

[ 49 ]                    4

The old the water clear will quaff,
  The young the pebbles flinging,
The children, each with merry laugh,
  Will pluck the flowers up-springing !'

' I will not tarry, the cottage near,
  Nor where the fountain's glowing ;
For mothers would see, by the water clear,
  Their children's tears down-flowing !
And wives would know their husbands dear,
  Nor would allow their going !'

J. S. BLACKIE.<br>H. C. LEONARD.

# ITALY.

*FROM THE LATIN OF SENECA* (A.D. 65).

## XXVIII.—THE END OF BEING.

THE end of being is to find out God!
And what is God?   A vast almighty Power,
Great and unlimited, whose potent will
Brings to achievement whatsoe'er He please.
He is all mind, His Being infinite—
All that we see, and all we do not see.
The Lord of heaven and earth, the God of Gods.
Without Him nothing is, yet what He is
We know not!   When we strive to comprehend
Our feeble guesses leave the most concealed.
To Him we owe all good we call our own.
To Him we live, to Him ourselves approve.
He is a Friend for ever at our side.
What cares He for the bleeding sacrifice?
O purge your hearts, and lead the life of good!
Not in the pride of temples made with stone
His pleasures lies, but in the piety
Of consecrated hearts, and lives devout.

H. C. LEONARD.

# ITALY.

*FROM THE MEDIAEVAL LATIN (EIGHTH CENTURY).*

## XXIX.—THE HEAVENLY JERUSALEM.

JERUSALEM, my happy home,
    When shall I come to thee ?
When shall my sorrows have an end ?
    Thy joys when shall I see ?

O happy harbour of the saints !
    O sweet and blessed soil !
In thee no sorrow may be found,
    No grief, no care, no toil.

In thee no sickness may be seen,
    No ache, no hurt, no sore ;
There is no death, nor ugly devil,
    But Life for evermore.

No dampish mist is seen in thee,
    No cold, nor darksome night ;
There every soul shines as the sun,
    There God Himself gives light.

There lust and lucre cannot dwell;
  There envy bears no sway;
There is no hunger, heat, nor cold,
  But pleasure every way.

Jerusalem! Jerusalem!
  God grant I once may see
Thy endless joys, and of the same
  Partaker aye may be!

Thy walls are made of precious stones;
  Thy bulwarks diamonds square;
Thy gates are of right orient pearl,
  Exceeding rich and rare.

Thy turrets and thy pinnacles
  With carbuncles do shine;
Thy very streets are paved with gold,
  Surpassing clear and fine.

Thy houses are of ivory;
  Thy windows crystal clear;
Thy tiles are made of burnished gold.
  O God that I were there!

Within thy gates nothing doth come
  That is not passing clean;
No spider's web, no dirt, no dust,
  No filth may there be seen.

Ah! my sweet home, Jerusalem,
  Would God I were in thee!
Would God my woes were at an end,
  Thy joys that I might see!

Thy saints are crowned with glory great ;
  They see God face to face ;
They triumph still, they still rejoice ;
  Most happy is their case !

We that are here in banishment
  Continually do moan ;
We sigh and sob, we weep and wail ;
  Perpetually we groan.

Our sweet is mixed with bitter gall ;
  Our pleasure is but pain ;
Our joys scarce last the looking on ;
  Our sorrows still remain.

But there they live in such delight,
  Such pleasure and such play,
As that to them a thousand years
  Doth seem as yesterday !

Thy vineyards and thy orchards are
  Most beautiful and fair :
Full furnishèd with trees and fruit
  Most wonderful and rare.

Thy gardens and thy gallant walks
  Continually are green ;
There grow such sweet and pleasant flowers
  As nowhere else are seen.

There's nectar and ambrosia made ;
  There's musk and civet sweet ;
There many a fair and dainty drug
  Are trodden under feet.

There cinnamon, there sugar, grows ;
    There nard and balm abound.
What tongue can tell, or heart conceive,
    The joys that there are found ?

Quite through the streets, with silent sound,
    The Flood of Life doth flow,
Upon whose banks, on every side,
    The Wood of Life doth grow.

There trees for evermore bear fruit,
    And evermore do spring ;
There evermore the angels sit,
    And evermore do sing.

There David stands, with harp in hand
    As master of the quire.
Ten thousand times that man were blest
    That might this music hear !

Our Lady sings *Magnificat*
    With tones surpassing sweet,
And all the virgins bear their part,
    Sitting about her feet.

*Te Deum* doth St. Ambrose sing ;
    St. Austin doth the like ;
Old Simeon and Zacharie
    Have not their songs to seek.

There Magdalen hath left her moan,
    And cheerfully doth sing
With blessed saints, whose harmony
    In every street doth ring.

Jerusalem, my happy home,
  Would God I were in thee !
Would God my woes were at an end,
  Thy joys that I might see !

ANON. (1601).

# ITALY.

*FROM THE ROMANCE VAUDOIS* (A.D. 1200).

## XXX.—THE WATCH-TOWER.

O FRIENDS beloved, arise from sleep !
    Christ's coming hour you cannot say.
To serve your God your vigils keep
    That you may reign in endless day.
O wait not for the gloomy night !
    Unhappy he who comes too late !
Nor bride nor Bridegroom shall invite
    His entrance to the precious gate.

A. MUSTON.

H. C. LEONARD.

# ITALY.

*FROM THE ITALIAN OF MICHAEL ANGELO* (A.D. 1515).

## XXXI.—INSPIRATION.

THE prayers I make will then be sweet indeed
   If Thou the Spirit give by which I pray ;
   My unassisted heart is barren clay,
Which, of its native self, can nothing feed.
Of good and pious works Thou art the seed,
   Which quickens only where Thou sayst it may ;
   Unless Thou show to us Thine own true way
No man can find it !   Father, Thou must lead !
Do Thou, then, breathe those thoughts into my mind
   By which such virtue may in me be bred
   That in Thy holy footsteps I may tread.
The fetters of my tongue do Thou unbind,
   That I may have the power to sing of Thee,
   And sound Thy praises everlastingly.

WORDSWORTH.

# SWITZERLAND.

*FROM THE ROMAUNSCH.*

## XXXII.—Jesus Only.

Up, up, my heart !
No more give way to sadness ;
  But know thou art
Redeemed to life and gladness.
  The secret, God long hid
In dark evangels,
  Now comes abroad
With trumpets of the angels.


The hidden morn,
With which time long went mother,
  At last is born ;
O Christ ! Thou, and no other,
  Comest to save
From sin and dark disgraces
  And, through Thy grave,
Show us sweet holy faces.

[ 59 ]

In Bethlehem, see
One born of woman lowly;
  Meek Virgin she,
In shadow of the Holy.
  But Him—O tell
Who towers in grandeur lonely?
  Earth, Heaven, and Hell
Make answer—'Jesus only.'


  Both God and man—
Unutterable wonder!
  In person one
In nature still asunder.
  Of our flesh, God
Disrobeth Himself never;
  And men, by blood,
His brothers are for ever.


  Who, with sore pain,
Death on the cross hath tasted,
  Our foes hath slain
And their black kingdom wasted.
  The while He lay
Bound in the grave's dark prison,
  Till the third day,
Behold the Conqueror risen!


  Him high Heaven holds,
With hands all pierced and bleeding,
  Which now He folds
For sinners interceding,

And shields us so
From Satan's fierce assaulting,
   When pilgrims go
Upon their journey halting.

   Up, then, my heart !
To Thee, my Jesus only,
   Till, when I part
On my last journey lonely,
   Safe from all harms
Thy blood shall shield me dying,
   Till in Thine arms
I wake to find me lying.

W. B. ROBINSON.

# HUNGARY.

*FROM THE MAGYAR OF JOHN KIS* (A.D. 1800).

## XXXIII.—THE PRAISE OF WISDOM.

GODDESS of thy votary's heart,
Wisdom, tell me where thou art !
Holy Virgin, in the throng
  Of mighty worlds I seek thy throne.
I seek thee, and have sought thee long,
  Of loveliest ones the loveliest one !
Right hand of the Deity !
  Graved in my heart thine image bright,
And the reflected ray from thee
  Makes nature's darkness melt in light.

The All-former's hidden works are known
  To thee, His everlasting will.
  Thou seest all upward mounting : still,
Still higher mounting to the throne
Where Good, pure Good, resides alone.
Thou seest the fires of discipline
Improve, subdue, correct, refine,
  Till, as the mists dissolve away
  In the diffusing smiles of day,
Man glides from mortal to divine.

[ 62 ]

Thou hallowed Goddess of my heart,
Tell me, tell me, where thou art !
Where thine eternal home, and say
May not my spirit wend its way
(For passionate longing might find pinions
To reach e'en thy sublime dominions)
To thine abode ?   Can naught but spirit
Thy presence seek, thy friendship merit ?
Why, struggling after thee, O why
Sink me in deep obscurity ?

Yet when, at morning dawn, I bring
  A matin incense to thine altar,
  When, though I scarcely breathe, but falter,
And, at the evening twilight, fling
My heart before thee, on the wing
  Of the calm breeze, methinks I hear
  Thy voice, O tell me art thou there ?
Methinks when, at the midnight hour,
  In solemn silence flitted by
The whisper that some viewless power
  Passes, in angel-chariot, nigh,
Methinks that whisper needs must be
Some herald's voice announcing thee !

SIR J. BOWRING.

# AUSTRIA.

*FROM THE BOHEMIAN OF JOHN KOLLAR* (A.D. 1790).

## XXXIV.—PARADISE.

KNOW'ST thou the land of Paradise above,
   The home of beauty and the seat of mind
Where virtue is the minister of love,
   Love, beauty, virtue, intellect enshrined,
All influential?  Where the breezes blow
   Odorous and mild, and nightingales from bowers
Of myrtles ceaseless sing, where palm-trees grow
   O'ershading, to protect, the sunny flowers?
Know'st thou the land where neither night nor heat
   Blacken or blast, no thorn the roses bear,
And pure desires their swift fruition meet,
Time's stream rolls on unhindered at time's feet?
   Wife, sister, each as other pure and dear,
   O mine for lasting ages!  Thou art there!

SIR J. BOWRING.

# GERMANY.

## XXXV.—A Christmas Carol.

A light from God throughout the welkin shone
And struck, with sudden ray, the field upon.
Then all the shepherds, full of fear and dread,
Beheld God's Mighty Angel overhead.
' Dread not,' he said, ' nor fear the heavenly light,
Glad news I bring you !   On this self-same night,
In David's city, your good Lord is come !
The blessed Child of God makes earth His home !
And, as a token that true words I've said,
The Lord of all lies bound, a crib His bed !'
Soon as the Angel's wondrous words were heard
A holy host of God's fair folk appeared.
From heavenly plains came down the angel throng
And this the burden of their joyful song,
' Love be there now to God in highest heaven,
And peace on earth to sons of men be given.'

H. C. Leonard.

# GERMANY.

*FROM THE FRANKISH (OLD HIGH GERMAN, TENTH CENTURY).*

## XXXVI.—A Good Bishop.

Before St. Anno
Six were sainted
Of our holy bishops.
Like the seven stars
They shall shine from heaven.
Purer and brighter
Is the light of Anno
Than a hyacinth set in a gold ring !

This darling man
We will have for a pattern ;
And those that would grow
In virtue and trustiness
Shall dress by him
As at a mirror.

As the sun in the air
Between earth and heaven
Glitters to both—
So went Bishop Anno

[ 66 ]

Between God and man.
Such was his virtue in the palace
That the Emperor obeyed him ;
He behaved with honour to both sides,
And was counted among the first barons.

In his gestures at worship
He was awful as an angel.
Many a man knew his goodness.
Hear what were his manners—
His words were frank and open ;
He spoke truth, fearing no man ;
Like a lion he sat among princes,
Like a lamb he walked among the people ;
To the unruly he was sharp ;
To the gentle he was mild ;
Widows and orphans
Praised him always.

Preaching and praying
No one could do better.
Happy was Cologne
To be worthy of such a bishop !

W. TAYLOR.

# GERMANY.

*FROM THE GERMAN OF GOETHE.*

## XXXVII.—THE ARCHANGELS' SONG.

### RAPHAEL.

THE sun, e'en as of old, is sounding
   With brother-spheres in rival song,
And, his predestined journey rounding,
   With thundering footstep rolls along.
Thy face new strength to angels lendeth,
   Though none its meaning fathom may;
Thy lofty works none comprehendeth,
   All glorious as on time's first day!

### GABRIEL.

And swift, with wondrous quickness fleeting,
   The beauteous earth spins round and round,
The glow of Paradise retreating
   Before the midnight's gloom profound;
Up o'er the rocks the foaming ocean
   Heaves from its deep primeval bed,
And rocks and seas, with endless motion,
   On, in the spheral sweep, are sped!

[ 68 ]

### MICHAEL.

And storms, in emulation raging,
  From sea to land, from land to sea,
Weave all around, a conflict waging,
  A chain of giant energy ;
And lurid desolations, blazing,
  Fore-run the volleyed thunder's way ;
Yet, Lord, Thy messengers are praising
  The mild procession of Thy day !

### THE THREE.

The sight new strength to angels lendeth,
  Though none Thy being fathom may !
Thy works no angel comprehendeth,
  All glorious as on time's first day !

VARIOUS.

# SPAIN.

*FROM THE SPANISH OF LOPE DE VEGA* (A.D. 1625).

## XXXVIII.—THE DOOR OF THE HEART.

LORD, what am I, that, with unceasing care,
   Thou didst seek after me, that Thou didst wait,
   Wet with unhealthy dews, before my gate,
And pass the gloomy nights of winter there?
O strange delusion! that I did not greet
   Thy blest approach; and O, to Heaven how lost
   If my ingratitude's unkindly frost
Has chilled the bleeding wounds upon Thy feet.
How oft my guardian angel gently cried,
   'Soul, from thy casement look, and thou shalt see
   How He persists to knock and wait for thee!'
And O! how often to that voice of sorrow,
   'To-morrow we will open,' I replied,
And when the morrow came I answered still, 'To-morrow.'

H. W. LONGFELLOW.

# SPAIN.

*FROM THE LEMOSIN, OR CATALONIAN, OF FORDI*
(A.D. 1220).

## XXXIX.—Contrarieties.

From day to day, I learn but to unlearn ;
   I live to die ; my pleasure is my woe ;
In dreary darkness I can light discern ;
   Though blind, I see ; and all but knowledge know.
I nothing grasp, and yet the world embrace ;
   Though bound to earth, to highest heaven I fly ;
With what's behind I run an untired race,
   And break from that which holds me mightily.


Evil I find, when hurrying after bliss ;
   Loveless, I love ; and doubt of all I see ;
All seems a dream that most substantial is ;
   I hate myself,—others are dear to me.
Voiceless, I speak ; I hear, of hearing void ;
   My aye is no ; truth becomes falsehood strange ;
I eat, not hungry ; shift, though unannoyed ;
   Touch without hands ; and sense to folly change.

I seek to soar, and then the deeper fall ;
  When most I seem to sink, then mount I still ;
Laughing, I weep ; and waking, dreams I call ;
  And when most cold, hotter than fire I feel.
Perplexed, I do what I would leave undone ;
  Losing, I gain ; time fleetest, slowliest flows ;
Though free from pain, 'neath pain's attacks I groan ;
  To craftiest fox, the gentlest lambkin grows.


Sinking, I rise ; and dressing, I undress ;
  The heaviest weight too lightly seems to fall ;
I swim,—yet rest in perfect quietness,
  And sweetest sugar turns to bitterest gall.
The day is night to me, and darkness day ;
  The time that's past is present to my thoughts ;
Strength becomes weakness ; hard is softest clay ;
  I linger, wanting what I wanted not.


I stand unmoved,—yet never, never stop,
  And what I seek not that besets me wholly ;
The man I trust not is my firmest prop ;
  The low is high,—the high seems ever lowly.
I chase what I can never hope to gain ;
  What's weak as sand-rope looks like firmest ground
The whirlpool seems a fountain's surface plain,
  And virtue but a weak and empty sound.
My songs are but an infant's uttering slow ;
  Disgusting in mine eyes is all that's fair ;
I turn, because I know not where to go ;
  I'm not at peace, but cannot war declare ;

And thus it is, and such is my dark doom,
   And so the world and so all nature fleets,
And I am curtained in the general gloom,
   And I must live, deceived by these deceits.

Let each apply what may to each belong,
   And, by these rules contrarious, wisely steer ;
For right oft flows from darkness covered wrong,
   And good may spring from seeming evil here.

H. W. LONGFELLOW.

# SPAIN.

*FROM THE GITANO.*

## XL.—The Deluge.

Now the Almighty, in the sky,
Holds His hand upraised on high.
Now the clouds begin to pour
Floods of water, more and more,
Down upon the world with might,
Never pausing day or night.
Now in terrible distress
All to God their cries address.
Now's the time of maddened rout,
Hideous cry, despairing shout ;
Of dear hope exists no gleam ;
Still the water down doth stream ;
Ne'er so little a creeping thing
But from out its hole doth spring :
See the mouse and see its mate
Scour along, nor stop nor wait ;
See the serpent and the snake
For the nearest highlands make ;
The tarantula I view,
Emmet small, and cricket too.

See the goat and bleating sheep ;
See the bull with bellowings deep,
And the rat with squealing shrill—
They have mounted on the hill.
See the stag, and see the doe,
How together fond they go !
Lion, tiger-beast, and pard
To escape are striving hard !
See the hare, how swift she runs,
Followed by her little ones ;
And the rabbit and the fox
Hurry over stones and rocks,
With the grunting hog, and horse,
Till at last they stop their course
On the summit of the hill.
All assembled, stand they still.
Soon, I ween, appeared in sight,
With them gathered on the height,
All with wings beneath the sky,
Bat and swallow, wasp and fly,
Gnat and sparrow, and behind
Comes the crow of carrion kind ;
Dove and pigeon are descried,
And the raven fiery-eyed,
With the beetle and the crane,
Flying on the hurricane.
See, they find no resting-place,
For the world's terrestrial space
Is with water covered o'er ;
Soon they'll sink to rise no more !
' To our father let us flee !'
Straight the ark-ship openeth he,

And, to everything that lives,
Kindly he admission gives.
All within he doth embark ;
Then, at once, he shuts the ark.
Everything therein has passed,
There he keeps them, safe and fast.

G. BORROW.

# SPAIN.

*FROM THE ANDALUSIAN.*

## XLI.—An Elegy on a Child.

WHITE roses crown her brow ;—mourn not thy loss,
   Sad mother !   Not with palm for conflict done,
   But pure and fair her innocent soul is gone,
And, on her breast, sweet flowers entwine her cross.

Her death was as the dreams of infants are ;
   Angels of light on her new waking smiled ;
   One only want she knows, this happy child,
One only want in heaven—till thou art there.

E. CHURTON.

# SPAIN.

*FROM THE CATALAN.*

## XLII.—An Evening Hymn.

Long is the night to him that waketh,
   Short is the night when sleep is sound ;
God grant us joy when morning breaketh;
   God send us rest while night goes round.

Soft as on bed of down new-driven,
   Sweet sleep, with heart at rest, be mine ;
And life, new life, shall dawn from heaven
   When morn's first eastern ray shall shine.

Look up, my soul ! thy God is near thee
   Who clothes the fields and guides each flower
That blooms or fades,—for He shall hear thee
   In joy, or sorrow's heaviest hour.

Thy drooping hope again shall flourish;
   The good day dimmed shall shine again ;
The times of tears more richly nourish
   Fresh seeds of gladness, sown in pain.

Hast thou done well? O, never, never
   Is goodness in this world alone !
A friend is thine no change can sever,
   Thy true heart, evermore thine own.·

An orphan thou mayst mourn to-morrow,
   For death on earth brings pain and thrall ;
Each heart must know its part of sorrow,
   But comfort waits alike for all !

One wretch alone no grace redeemeth ;
   One groans all comfortless alone.—
Woe, woe to him who none esteemeth,
   Whose sullen heart is warmed to none !

Children of God, whate'er betide you
   In life or death like brothers still
Grieve not, for good to-day denied you
   Wait the good hour, for come it will !

Long is the night to him that waketh ;
   Short is the night when sleep is sound ;
God grant us joy when morning breaketh ;
   God shield our rest while night goes round.

                E. CHURTON.

# PORTUGAL.

## *FROM THE PORTUGUESE OF LUIS DE CAMOENS*
### (A.D. 1569).

### XLIII.—THE NOBLER LIFE.

SINCE, in this dreary vale of tears,
No certainty but death appears,
Why should we waste our vernal years
    In hoarding useless treasure ?

No, let the young and ardent mind
Become the friend of human-kind,
And, in the generous service, find
    A source of purer pleasure.

Better to live despised and poor
Than guilt's eternal stings endure !
The future smile of God shall cure
    The wound of earthly woes.

Vain world ! did we but rightly feel
What ills thy treacherous charms conceal,
How would we long from thee to steal
    To death and sweet repose !

UNKNOWN.

# ·FRANCE.

*FROM THE LANGUE D'OIL, OR ROMANCE WALLON*
(A.D. 1150).

## XLIV.—A Visit to Paradise.

AND now the angel led them on
Where Paradise in beauty shone,
And there they saw the land all full
Of woods and rivers beautiful,
And meadows large, besprent with flowers,
And scented shrubs in fadeless bowers,
And trees with blossom fair to see,
And fruit which, most deliciously,
Hung from the boughs.   Nor briar, nor thorn,
Thistle, nor blighted tree forlorn,
With blackened leaf, was there ; for spring
Displayed a year-long blossoming.
And never shed their leaf the trees,
Nor failed their fruit ; and still the breeze
Blew soft, scent-laden from the leas.
There the clear sun knew no declining,
Nor fog nor mist obscured his shining,
No cloud across that sky did stray,
Taking the sun's sweet light away.

Nor cutting blast nor blighting air,
For bitter winds blew never there.
Nor heat, nor frost, nor pain, nor grief,
Hunger nor thirst ; for swift relief
From every ill was there.   Plenty
Of every good, right easily,
Each had according to his will ;
And ever wandered, blithely still,
In large and pleasant pastures green,
O ! such as earth hath never seen !

S. DE SISMONDI.
T. ROSCOE.

# FRANCE.

*FROM THE LANGUE D'OC, OR ROMANCE PROVENÇAL, OF PEYROLS* (A.D. 1193).

## XLV.—A Crusader's Song.

I HAVE seen the Jordan river,
   I have seen the holy grave;
Lord, to Thee my thanks I render,
   For the joys Thy goodness gave,
Showing to my raptured sight
Where Thou first didst see the light.

Vessel good, and favouring breezes,
   Pilot trusty, soon shall we
See again the towers of Marseilles
   Rising o'er the briny sea.
Farewell, Acre! farewell, all
Of Temple or of Hospital!

Now, alas! the world's decaying!
   When shall we again behold
Kings like lion-hearted Richard,
   France's monarch, stout and bold,
Montserrat's good Marquis, or
The Empire's glorious Emperor?

Ah ! Lord God, if You believed me
   You would pause in granting powers
Over cities, kingdoms, empires,
   Over castles, towns, and towers,
For the men that powerful be
Pay the least regard to Thee !

S. DE SISMONDI.<br>T. ROSCOE.

# FRANCE.

*FROM THE FRENCH OF LAMARTINE.*

## XLVI.—ODE TO THE WORD.

WORD uncreated ! fruitful spring
    Of justice and of liberty !
Speech that to earth doth healing bring !
    O living ray of verity !
And is it true Thy voice, from age to age obeyed,
No longer now hath power to lend its guiding aid,
Like to a sound far off, that, spreading, dies away ?
    And that a voice of wider reach,
    The voice of merely human speech,
For ever drowns what Thou dost say ?

But reason !—'tis Thyself !  What was this reason then
  Before the hour when Thou didst turn its night to day ?
Cloud, doubt, obscurity, contention, systems vain,
  Torch carried by our pride to lead our steps astray !

The world was sunk in gloomy night,
  And doctrines without faith struggled like billows high,
Deceived and undeceived by their funereal light,
  Man's spirit, drowned in chaos, floated helpless by ;

And hope and fear by turns, according to their mood,
  Dispeopled heaven, or filled again its vacant throne,
Imposture grew and throve on sacrificial blood,
  A thousand gods declared the gods by men unknown !
        Search in Palmyra's barren sands,
        Search in Osiris' slimy clay,
        In pantheons of ancient lands
Where breathe the baneful shades of gods proscribed
    to-day !
        Draw from the mire or grassy mound
Gods molten, graven, shaped of plastic clay,
These mutilated monsters, symbols of decay,
And say what was indeed this reason so profound
        When she adored such wrecks as they !
Nor did earth's wisdom know an exploit from a crime,
The names for praise and blame as from an urn were spilt,
And human glory satisfied the child of time,
        And virtues thought the most sublime
        Were oft in truth but vices gilt !

           Thou comest, and Thy word
           Flies, as of old 'twas heard,
             And made black chaos fly ;
           From night it drew the morn,
             Divided sea from sky,
           From number then was born
             Both rest and harmony !
           Thy word creative darts,
           Virtues from vices parts,
             And truth from specious lie ;
           The master justice learns,
             The slave gains liberty,
           The poor content discerns,

The rich learn charity !
Our Father, God, and Guide,
In whom the just confide,
    To mortal men draws near !
The prayer that wins His ear
Floats upward, free and clear,
    On wings without a stain
    From rites of blood and pain !
Our sins and ill desires,
The thoughts that passion fires,
These victims He requires,
    And these His altars gain !
And now the immortal beam
    Darts beyond time its ray ;
Through hope's celestial dream
The moments shorter seem
    Of exiled man's brief stay ;
Celestial mercy's stream
    Bears heaviest griefs away ;
Eternal day begins
    With its peace-bringing light,
Repentance pardon wins ;
    And faith is turned to sight
For sage and child to-day !
    And man, his burden gone,
    Rests on that word alone
Since dawned the Gospel ray !

The soul, when once enlightened by Thy law Divine,
  Within the moral sphere where ·Thou dost guide our
    eyes,
Discovers, all at once, more novel virtues shine
  Than when the daring glass of Herschell swept the skies

And led the astonished sight in the celestial ways;
Nor do the eyes which nightly search, with eager gaze,
    See new stars multiply and on the vision rise.
And never from those fires which roll, in orbit vast,
Never from Sinai's mount when kindled by the blast,
Nor yet from awful Horeb, great Jehovah's throne,
    Hath light on eyes of mortals shone
So living and so fruitful as the truth which first,
With sudden dawning, on the darkened nations burst
    From Calvary's sacred hill alone !


The star which to Thy cot the Magian sages led,
The light which brought the shepherds to Thy cradle-bed
    To see their God all crowned with indigence and scorn,
Hath on the grateful earth unfading daylight shed,
A light that every age in turn hath worshippèd,
Which in the night of time with constant oil is fed,
    And shall not wane when skies grow dim at judgement
        morn !


And yet they say this star is veiled and fades away,
The light of this proud age hath overcome its ray,
    The world, grown older now, no more of Thee hath
        need !
Reason alone immortal and Divine, they say !
The rust of time hath brought Thy doctrine to decay,
And now, from off Thy ruined fane, from day to day,
    Some falling marble tells that faith in Thee is dead.


O Christ, it is too true ! for Thine eclipse is come !
The earth upon Thy star hath cast its shadowy gloom,

In this our age all falls before our sorrowing sight,
Of twenty centuries fallen the dust all mingled lies,
The darkness and the light, fables and verities,
In dire confusion float before our puzzled eyes,
    And one saith, ' 'Tis the day !' another, ' 'Tis the night !'


E'en as a ray of heaven that pierces through the haze,
In traversing the mire and night of ancient days,
    Thy word has suffered from our profanations !
The human eye impure would soil the solar beam !
Imposture vain has dimmed the very truth supreme,
And tyrants, making of Thy faith a diadem,
    Have gilded with Thy name the yoke of nations !
But as the lightning flash which, falling on the glade,
Regains the firmament, unaltered by its shade,
    So man can never soil Thy law of verity !
His ignorance doth often dim Thy light sublime,
His hatred oft confounds Thy virtue and our crime,
Flatterers to tyrants sell Thy precepts oftentime,
    And still Thy word is justice, love, and liberty !


But reason blind demands what signs and miracles
Attest that ancient law's neglected oracles ?
    The miracle is there, and without end shall shine,
In that the heavenly truth, in spite of falsehood's lure,
In that the shining torch, in spite of shade obscure,
In that the sacred word, in spite of lips impure,
    Hath passed two thousand years and still is found
        Divine !


But there are shadows ?   Yet, O torch of life's long day,
Thou hast not promised stars to shine with cloudless ray,

Nor hath the eye of man been made for light all pure ;
No earthly day can pass from shadow wholly free ;
God veils His proper splendour that the earth may see.
By contrast only with the night of mystery
   The eye can see the day, and man the truth endure.


A century is born, and cries of hope ascend ;
The human race, deceived, sees dream with dream contend ;
   Opinions, dogmas, ebb and flow with ceaseless roar,
A hundred years, and Time, like vapours vanishing,
Rolls them to quick oblivion 'neath his rapid wing ;
And, when his broom away the barren dust doth fling,
   What of the century remains ?   One lie the more !


The age when Thou wast born can never know decay,
It shines above us still as an eternal day ;
   One half of time grows pale before its lustrous power,
The other half receives the light which Thou hast brought ;
Two  thousand  changeful  years  exhaust  their  shallow
      thought,
Yet not a word of Thine can ever come to naught,
   And from Thy cradle truth computes her natal hour !


In vain would thankless man, too weary to believe,
   From broken altars and from memory's fading gleam,
   Attempt to banish Thee as some unwelcome dream ;
Still dost Thou reign within, although without his leave,
And from a distant past all gleaming with Thy praise,
Thy splendour Thou dost shed to earth's remotest days !
Light of our souls, whene'er Thou palest they grow pale !
Basis of states, whene'er Thou failest they must fail !
   Sap of the human race, if Thou art gone it dries !

Root of our laws, implanted deep within the ground,
  Where'er Thou languishest our virtue quickly dies,
  Each fibre in our hearts to Thy great name replies,
In every place Thou livest again in thought profound,
    E'en in the senseless hatred found
    Of him who now Thy name decries !

    O beacon raised upon the shore,
      Unblasted by the storms of time,
    The lights of ages, evermore,
      Are centred in Thy ray sublime !
    And, hallowing human memory,
    Thou guid'st the eyes of history
    Up to the source whence all things flow !
      The mystery of the weak is plain,
      And why all worlds the strife maintain
    'Twixt endless life and mortal woe !

    Thy power no more is the caprice
      Alike of demagogues and kings :
    It is eternal righteousness
      Reflected in the laws it brings !
    Thy virtue is no more a dream,
    Fed by vain hopes and self-esteem,
    Problem of pride and human fame !
      It is the noble offering
      Of human wills, that service bring
    To the eternal will, and name !

    Thy truth no more a prism shall be,
      Where every error is at home,
    The light which springs from sophistry
      And vanishes like flecks of foam !

A ray of the eternal morn
Pure, fruitful, for all ages born,
To every child of man it flies ;
   Sublime equality of souls,
   For sages, flames and thunder-rolls,
For children, veils for tender eyes !

Food which the spirit's life supplies,
   Heat whose bright ray is God indeed,
Germ which believes and fructifies,
   Thy word in every place the seed !
Truth that can touch all mental states,
Which love divine communicates
From heart to heart, from eye to eye !
   And though no uttered words proceed,
   Good actions are its holy creed,
And virtues are its majesty !

All instincts to Thy yoke engage,
   Man's birth, life, death with Thee are found ;
Each of his years of pilgrimage
   By faith in Thee, O Christ, is bound !
Suffering, his tears are offered Thee ;
Happy, his best prosperity
Unblessed by Thee is held unblessed ;
   And, when the hour of death is come,
   Armed with Thy words he meets the gloom,
The shadow of eternal rest !

When man's brief day of life is spent
   His memory Thou dost safely guard,
And fastenest to his monument
   The broken links that time had marred ;

No more the drops from sorrowing eyes
Wet the cold stone where friendship lies,
But, watered by those loving tears,
 Prayer, highest union of hearts,
 Peace to the much-loved dead imparts,
Hope to the living mourner bears !

Of every sacrifice the meed,
 Each one is fed by faith in Thee ;
In every sad and woful need
 To Thee turns poor humanity!
And if I ask each loving dole,
Each tear which would my grief console,
Each generous pardon that is shown,
 Each humble virtue that we scan,
In whose great name console you man ?
They answer me, ' In His alone !'

'Tis Thou whose tenderest pity sends
 Sweet charity with generous load,
And guides the blind, and kindly tends
 The needy traveller on the road ;
 'Tis Thou who, in the wretched home
Where this world's outcasts sadly come
In tears and suffering to lie,
 To age sends holy ministries,
 To nameless ones gives families,
And to the sick a place to die !

Thou livest in relics of the past,
 In temples standing or o'erthrown,
In altars, churches, columns vast ;
 All in the past is Thine alone !

And all that man doth still upraise,
All dwellings that re echo praise,
All in the future is for Thee !
 The centuries no dust can own,
 The hills contain no fossiled stone,
That carries not Thy memory !

In fine, O vast and mighty thought,
 More than the mind can entertain :
All souls are filled and inly wrought
 With Thy great name, invoked in vain !
By doubts funereal still self-bound,
Man vainly heaps the darkness round,
E'er followed by Thy splendour bright !
 And, like the all-enlightening day,
 The world can ne'er escape its ray
Except by plunging into night !

And dost Thou die ? Thy faith, as in a cloudy bed,
Beneath the horizon of the age is vanishèd,
Like to a sun lost from the place in which it shone,
Of which men whisper, ' It was there, but it is gone !'
And our descendants, in the far-off future time,
Will link their fable with Thy holy truths sublime ?
And of the Crucified will speak in time to come
As of the lying gods who at Thy voice were dumb,
Who bore the thunderbolt or wand of magic fame,
Dreams at the memory of which we blush with shame ?
But all these gods, O Christ ! as yet have nothing brought
Except a deeper shadow to our darkened thought.
 But of delirious dreams the base and shameful sign,
It shrinks away at the first sound of words of Thine.

But Thou didst come to sit upon their shattered throne,
The God of truth, and grace, and virtue Thou alone !
Their laws betray themselves before Thy law supreme !
But where the virtues which could nobler seem ?
To eclipse Thy day what other day could shine ?
Thou who didst fill their place, who could succeed to
    Thine ?
Who knows if this dark shade wherein Thy doctrine pales
Is real decay, or heaven-sent night that only veils :
Some transient cloud that soon will part in twain,
Whence faith, transfigured, soon shall mount and rise again,
As in Thine earthly life, when lowly and mis-known,
Thou wast transfigured, and in clouds Thy glory shone,
When Thy divinity resumed its heavenly flight,
And flowed from Thee to clothe Mount Tabor's lonely
    height,
When without wings it poised Thee in the upper air,
Dazed the astonished eyes of Thy disciples there,
And, to console them for Thy near and sad farewell,
Though man about to die, revealed Thee God as well !


Yes, by whatever name the future calleth Thee,
We hail Thee God ! for only man Thou canst not be !
Nor had man ever found, in his infirmity,
This germ divinely-given of immortality,
Day in the gloomy night, virtue in midst of vice,
In narrow selfishness the thirst for sacrifice !
In fiercest conflict, peace : hope in grief's sorest smart,
In rebel pride itself humility of heart,
Hate in the midst of love, and pardon in offence,
And in repentant tears a second innocence !

To worth so great as this our incense shall ascend,
And to its virtues shall our faith adoring bend!


Refuge of ignorance,
  Thy truths of mystery
Are shrines of hopes that glance
  And soar beyond the sky!
Thine ethics, chaste and sweet,
Perfume the pure retreat
With peace and grace and love;
  The atmosphere we find
  Is scented like the wind
That rose from Eden's grove!


When human nature bends
  To take Thy service free
She pure becomes, ascends
  And grows divine in Thee!
And all vain thoughts elate,
Aimed high as mortal fate,
Rise from the burdened heart;
  And man, the child of light,
  Returns from paths of night
To find the better part!


The heart's true peace is come;
  The soul is one long sigh;
All vain desires are dumb,
  Merged in a purpose high!
And peace and pleasure new,
Eternal life in view,

Bring full serenity !
And Christian lives entire,
Like one long prayer aspire !
An acted hymn, in praise of immortality !

And virtues the most rare,
By stoics hardly won,
The humble habits are
Women and children own !
The earth, transfigured quite,
A pathway of delight
Where pleasant shade is given,
Where man in man doth recognise
A brother, and to God, ' My Father !' cries ;
And all steps lead to heaven.

O Thou who once that second glorious dawn didst bring,
Whose second chaos saw harmonious order spring,
O Word who, with the truth, didst bring from heaven above
Justice, and tolerance, and liberty, and love !
For ever reign, O Christ ! over the human mind,
And be the link divine which man to God doth bind !
Illumine without end with all Thy fire sublime
The centuries asleep within the womb of time !
And may Thy name, bequeathed, a matchless heritage,
To child from mother down descend from age to age,
Long as the eye at night shall for the daylight pine,
The heart for immortality and hope divine,—
Long as humanity, all desolate and pale,
With tears shall sadly water this terrestrial vale,
Long as the virtues shall their guarded altars grace,
Or keep their names unchanged amongst our mortal race !

7

For me, whether Thy name revives or sinks in gloom,
God of my cradle, be the God, too, of my tomb !
The darker grows the night, the feebler grow mine eyes
The more they seek the torch which paleth in the skies ;
And if the broken altar whence the crowd hath passed
Should fall on me !—O temple to my heart so dear,
Temple where I have learnt all truth that I revere,—
Still would I clasp thy one remaining column fast,
And crushed beneath thy sacred dust would perish there !

H. C. LEONARD.

# FRANCE.

*FROM THE BASQUE OF CAMOUSSARY.*

## XLVII.—The Passing Bell.

As from mountains to the sea
    Flows the rapid river,
So I march—unhappy me !
    To the tomb for ever.
Now 'tis past—my life is past,
    Lot of every mortal !
Now my trembling feet must haste
    To the gloomy portal.


As the wolf, with sudden spring,
    Some poor lambkin rendeth,
As the vulture on the wing
    On the dove descendeth,
So the cruel grasp of death
    Stills my heart within me.
Ah ! my last entreating breath
    Cannot respite bring me !

[ 99 ]

7—2

Now my pulse is weaker grown,
    Heart is nothing stronger,
I can scarce, without a groan,
    Feel my breathing longer.
Lord, receive my soul, I pray,
    To Thy presence fleeting !
Now I go my lonesome way—
    Take, O friends, my greeting.

Now the solemn passing toll
    Sounds in earnest pleading,
Spreads the tidings that a soul
    Death is captive leading.
May my soul now upwards fly
    To the land of blessing,
Happy, if her lot to die
    God's own peace possessing.

FRANCESQUE MICHEL.
H. C. LEONARD.

# FRANCE.

*FROM THE BRETON OF A. L. JENKINS.*

## XLVIII.—THE GREATEST TREASURE.

In the Gospel I have won
All I sought beneath the sun ;
Now the riches of the earth
I esteem of little worth.

> O most precious Treasure,
> Giving endless pleasure !
> Hearts to God we lift
> For His grandest gift.

As I walked in darksome ways—
Like St. Paul in ancient days—
Light from Heaven illumed the road,
Led me to the Word of God.

Now another man am I ;
Beats my heart with pleasure high ;
Light instead of darkness reigns ;
Life instead of death remains.

In the Gospel word, at length,
Found have I the source of strength ;
Earth and Heaven are reconciled ;
God my Father—I His child.

Earthly days go swiftly by,
But His word can never die ;
Sweet the promise is to me—
'Where I am thou too shalt be.'

What devotion can I render
For a love so strong and tender ?
Him while I am following
All day long my heart shall sing :

O most precious Treasure
Giving endless pleasure !
Hearts to God we lift
For His grandest gift.
                        A. L. Jenkins.
                        H. C. Leonard.

# ASIA.

# PALESTINE.

*FROM THE HEBREW OF ISAIAH THE YOUNGER*
(B.C. 536).

## XLIX.—THE MISSION OF THE ANOINTED.

BEHOLD, my Servant shall deal prudently,
Exalted shall he be, and set on high.
Even as many were surprised at thee,
(So marred his visage more than any man,
So marred his form more than the sons of men),
Thus shall he startle nations in surprise;
The kings of earth shall shut their mouths at him :
Since what had not been told them they have seen,
And what they had not heard they have perceived.
    Who hath believed the message, and to whom
Was shown the ETERNAL'S arm ?   For he up-grew
Before Him, as a soft and tender sprout,
And as a shoot from out a barren soil ;
No form had he nor comeliness, nor his
The beauty that, when seen, attracts the eye.
Of men rejected and despised, a man
Of sorrows, and acquainted with all grief.
As one from whom one hides his face was he ;
He was despised, and we esteemed him not.
    Surely he took our griefs, our sorrows bore,
Yet we supposed him smitten by his God.

But he was wounded for our sins, was bruised
For our iniquities, the chastisement
Of peace, for us obtained, was laid on him,
And with his wounds were we completely healed.
All we like wandering sheep had gone astray ;
We turned, each one of us, to his own way ;
The ETERNAL laid on him the sins of all !

He his oppressions bore with lowly heart,
And opened not his mouth ; he as a lamb
Is brought to slaughter, as a sheep is dumb
Before her shearers, opened not his mouth.
In condemnation he was led along ;
And who considered that from out the land
Where dwell the living he was torn away,
For the transgressions of my people stricken ?

His grave beside the wicked was assigned,
His death was with the proud, although he did
No wrong, and in his mouth was found no guile.
Yet the ETERNAL chose to bruise him sore,
And give him grief.   But when his soul shall make
An offering for sin, he shall behold
A seed, he shall prolong his lengthening days,
And in his hand the ETERNAL'S will shall reign.
The travail of his soul shall yield its fruit :
This shall he see, well-pleased ; knowledge of him,
My righteous Servant, shall make many just,
Since he hath borne away their trespasses.
So with the great will I divide to him,
And with the strong he shall divide the spoil,
Because in death he hath outpoured his soul,
While yet he bore the sins of multitudes,
And for transgressors intercession made.

H. C. LEONARD.

# PALESTINE.

*FROM THE SAMARITAN* (A.D. 60).

### L.—A Hymn of Gerizim.

No God is there but one,
  The everlasting God,
He who for ever lives,
  Omnipotent is He.

In Thy great power we trust ;
  Thou only art our Lord,
For Thou from earliest time
  Hast led creation on.

Thy power was hid from men,
  Thy glory and Thy love.
Revealed are things revealed !
  Revealed the unrevealed !

E. Deutsch.

# PALESTINE.

*FROM THE ARAMAIC* (A.D. 427).

### LI. — ABRAM'S SEARCH FOR GOD.

ABRAM, says the ancient story,
    Wandered in the fields abroad,
Seeking, in creation's glory,
    Where to find the only God.

Wistfully on all things gazing,
    Lifted he his eyes on high,
Saw the star of evening, blazing
    Brilliant in the fading sky.

' This is God !' he cried, admiring,
    But he looked again, and soon
All its lustre was expiring,
    Vanquished by the rising moon !

Up she rose, in radiance shining,
    ' This,' said he, ' is God, at least !'
Soon he marked her light declining,
    For the sunrise filled the east.

Now the golden orb, ascending,
  Ran his race with joyful speed ;
Abram cried, before it bending,
  ' Surely this is God indeed !'

But the glorious rays, beclouded,
  Soon with lessened lustre shone :
Darkness all the landscape shrouded,
  Sun, and moon, and stars were gone !

Home returning, sad and lonely,
  Abram soon the secret knew :
' Ye and I are creatures only
  Of the living God and true !

' All your glory and your splendour
  Are but shadows of His throne :
I my praise will ever render
  To the God of heaven alone !'

                H. POLANO.
                H. C. LEONARD.

# PALESTINE.

*MISHNAIC HEBREW* (1st century a.d.)

From the SHEMONEH ESREH, or Daily Prayers.

## LII.—DAILY PRAYERS.

BLESSED art Thou, O Lord, our God and the God of our fathers, the Most High God.

Thou art holy and Thy name is holy, and the saints daily praise Thee.

Thou graciously impartest knowledge to man, and teachest to mortals reason.

Cause us to turn, O our Father, to Thy law, and draw us near, O our King, to Thy service.

Forgive us, our Father, for we have sinned; pardon us, our King, for we have transgressed.

Ready to pardon and forgive art Thou; Blessed art Thou, O Lord most gracious, who dost abundantly pardon.

Look, we beseech Thee, upon our afflictions, and redeem us speedily for Thy Name's sake, for a mighty redeemer Thou art.

Return to Jerusalem, Thy city, with compassion, and dwell therein as Thou hast promised.

Rebuild her speedily, in our days, a structure everlasting; and establish therein the throne of David.

O that our eyes may behold Thy return to Zion with mercy. Blessed art Thou, O Lord, who restorest Thy glory unto Zion.

Blessed art Thou, O Lord, who hearest prayer. Hear our voice, O Lord our God, and accept with favour these our prayers.

We praise Thee, for Thou art the Lord our God, and the God of our fathers for ever and ever, the Rock of our Life, the Shield of our salvation.

Thou art good, for Thy mercies fail not; and compassionate, for Thy lovingkindness never ceaseth; our hopes are for ever in Thee.

And all that live shall give thanks unto Thee for ever, and shall praise Thy name in truth, the God of our salvation and our aid for ever.

Arranged by GAMALIEL II.

# PALESTINE.

*TALMUDIC HEBREW.*

## LIII.—Elijah in the Market-place.

An orient city, in the glare
   Of morning sunshine, and the street
   Is trod by crowds of busy feet;
The hum of commerce fills the air.

Each group contends for mammon's prize
   And cries its wares, with voices loud;
   A stranger stands amid the crowd
And watches them, with wistful eyes.

His robe is wrought of camels' hair,
   A pilgrim's staff is in his hand,
   One man alone beholds him stand
Amongst the people passing there.

But, to this one, the stranger's guise
   Recalls the ' burning shining light '
   Which rose in Israel's darkest night !
So gazes he, with awed surprise.

[ 112 ]

' O stranger, tell thy name I pray !
   Fain would I linger near thy side !
   Art thou Elijah (then he cried)
Who comes before the Lord's great day ?'

The stranger took the inquirer's hand :
   ' My name to thee I need not tell,
   Thy faithful heart has judged me well :
Elijah doth before thee stand !

' Yet by my side thou must not be,
   Not here my message can be given ;
   But, ere again I enter heaven,
One question thou may'st ask of me.'

A moment's silent thought, and then
   The question came : ' O tell me, pray,
   Who may abide the Lord's great day
Of all this thronging crowd of men ?'

A warder from a neighbouring prison
   Along the street that moment passed :
   ' This man,' Elijah said, ' at last
Will stand as one beloved of heaven !'

The warder heard, and stood amazed :
   ' A simple man,' said he, ' am I !'
   ' I know thee,' was the quick reply,
' In heaven thy daily acts are praised !

' Ever, with gentle deeds of love,
   Thou to thy prisoners bring'st relief,
   Pitying their woes and hopeless grief.
Such kindly deeds are praised above !'

8

Two working men next hastened by ;
  ' These two,' Elijah cried, ' are blest,
  Favoured of heaven above the rest !'
This heard, they both astonished cry :

' We work but at our daily trade,
  A humble handicraft is ours !
  To earn our bread takes all our powers,
No claim have we to saintly grade !'

' I know you well !' the Seer exclaims ;
  ' Where sorrow falls your voice is heard ;
  You heal each strife with kindly word,
Peace and goodwill your constant aims.

Such the Lord loves !   In life's highway
  Who heals the sad and lonely heart—
  Who always takes the peaceful part—
These shall abide the Lord's great Day !'

Midst human woe and human strife
  Learn thou, O man, the secret high—
  To count, in all simplicity,
The law of love the law of life.

                E. DEUTSCH.
                H. C. LEONARD.

# PALESTINE.

*FROM THE ARABIZED HEBREW OF ELAZAR HA-KALIR*
(8TH CENTURY A.D.).

## LIV.—THE GLAD TIDINGS.

THE voice of Elijah, who bringeth glad tidings, and saith :

Thy salvation will I confirm when the Messiah cometh. It is the voice of my Beloved coming :

> And I will declare the glad tidings.

It is the voice of Him that cometh with myriads of saints, standing on the Mount of Olives :

> And I will declare the glad tidings.

It is the voice of the Messiah when He cometh at the sound of the great trumpet, when the mountain will divide :

> And I will declare the glad tidings.

It is the voice of my Beloved who knocketh, and shineth forth from Seir, and the mountains of the east shall divide :

> And I will declare the glad tidings.

It is the voice of Elijah proclaiming redemption, and the Messiah coming with all His holy ones with Him :

> And I will declare the glad tidings.

It is the voice of the Bathkol thundering from Zion, proclaiming freedom to the whole world :

And I will declare the glad tidings.

It is the voice of salvation proclaiming the welcome time of the earth's acknowledging the One-ness of His Name :

And I will declare the glad tidings.

It is the voice of the Mighty One of heaven and earth exclaiming: ' Can a nation be born in a day ?'

And I will declare the glad tidings.

It is the voice proclaiming the time of redemption, when the people shall see light, and it shall come to pass that at evening time there shall be light :

And I will declare the glad tidings.

It is the voice to make glad the Rose of Sharon; for they shall rise who sleep in Hebron :

And I will declare the glad tidings.

It is the voice of the Man whose name is the Branch :

And I will declare the glad tidings.

It is the voice proclaiming : ' Arise from the dust, awake, and sing ye who dwell in the dust ':

And I will declare the glad tidings.

It is the voice of granting salvation to His people for ever, even to David, and to his children for evermore.

J. W. ETHERIDGE.

# PALESTINE.

*FROM THE MODERN HEBREW.*

## LV.—Worship Song.

Before Thy heavenly Word revealed
    the wonders of Thy will,
Before the earth and heavens came forth
    from chaos deep and still,
E'en then Thou reignest Lord supreme,
    as Thou wilt ever reign,
And moved Thy Holy Spirit o'er
    the dark unfathomed main.


But when, through all the empty space,
    Thy mighty voice was heard,
Then darkness fled, and heavenly light
    came beaming at Thy word ;
All nature then proclaimed Thee King,
    most blessed and adored !
The great Creator, God alone,
    the universal Lord !

[ 117 ]

And when this vast created world
    returns to endless night,
When heaven and earth shall fade away
    at thy dread word of might,
Still Thou in majesty wilt rule
    Almighty One alone,
Great God with mercy infinite,
    on Thy exalted throne.


Immortal Power !   Eternal One,
    with Thee what can compare ?
Thy glory shines in heaven and earth
    and fills the ambient air.
All time, all space, by Thee illumed,
    grows bright and brighter still,
Obedient to Thy high behest,
    and to Thy heavenly will.


To Thee dominion sole belongs,
    and 'tis to Thee alone
My Father, Saviour, Living God,
    I make my sorrows known ;
Thy love celestial and divine,
    descends upon my heart,
Inspiring courage, hope, and joy,
    and bidding grief depart.


Protected by Thy boundless love
    my body sinks to rest ;
My soul, within Thy heavenly arm,
    reposes, calm and blest.

Lord of my life ! in darkest night
  I sleep and have no fear,
And in the early dawn of day
  I wake and find Thee near.

MRS. JULIUS COLLINS.

# SYRIA.

*FROM THE MOABITE OF KING MESHA* (II. KINGS iii, 4).

## LVI.—Moab's Boast.

I, Mesha, King of Moab, erected this stone to Chemosh.
A stone of salvation, for he saved me from all despoilers
And made me see my desire on all my enemies,
Even on Omri, King of Israel.
Now they afflicted Moab many days,
For Chemosh was angry with his land.
His son (Ahab) succeeded him,
And he also said : ' I will afflict Moab.'
In my days Chemosh said :—
' Let us go, and I will see my desire on him and his house,
And I will destroy Israel with an everlasting destruction.'
Now the King of Israel had fortified himself in Ataroth,
And I assaulted the city, and captured it,
And I slew all the warriors thereof,
For the well-pleasing of Chemosh and of Moab.
And I took away thence the vessels of Jehovah,
And I offered them before Chemosh.
And Chemosh said to me :—
' Go take Nebo from Israel.'

And I went by night, and fought against it from dawn to
    noon,
And I took it, and slew in all seven thousand men,
And I took away thence the vessels of Jehovah,
And I offered them before Chemosh.

F. KLEIN.

# SYRIA.

## LVII.—A ROYAL EPITAPH.

I AM carried away ;
The time of my non-existence has come ;
My spirit has disappeared,—
Like the day on which I became silent,
Since which I have become mute.

I am lying in this coffin,
In the tomb which I built,
O thou who readest, remember this—
Let none of royal race, let no other man
Open my funeral chamber !
Let no one seek for treasure here !
Let no one move my coffin,
Nor molest me in this funeral bed !
For such shall have no rest below,
Nor shall they have fruit above,
Nor living form under the sun !

For, by the grace of the god, I am carried away ;
The time of my non-existence has come ;
My spirit has disappeared !

JULES OPPERT.

# SYRIA.

*FROM THE SYRIAC OF SAINT EPHRAEM*
(A.D. 350).

## LVIII.—A PENITENTIAL CRY.

BEFORE my sins
In dread array
Disclose my shame
On Thy great day,
And from Thy face
I shrink away,
Have mercy on me, gracious Lord, I humbly pray !

Ere yet is closed
On me Thy door,
O Son of God,
Whose threshing-floor
Shall then be fired
And quenched no more,
Have mercy on me, gracious Lord, I Thee implore !

Before the wheel
Of time is broke
Above the fount
Where drink all folk,
And pitcher falls
At Thy swift stroke,
Thy mercy on me, gracious Lord, I now invoke !

Ere they whose faith
Is counterfeit
Their sentence wait
Before Thy seat,
And Thy ' Depart !'
With wonder meet,
Have mercy on me, gracious Lord, I Thee intreat !


Before Thine host
Thou dost forth-send,
From east to west
Their flight to wend,
To gather all
That do offend,
Thy mercy to me, gracious Lord, do Thou extend !


Ere yet my dust
Returns to clay
As once it was !
And to decay
All beauteous forms
Pass swift away,
Thy mercy to me, gracious Lord, do Thou display !


Before the blast
Of death doth blow,
As on a tree
No more to grow,
And fell disease
Doth lay me low,
Thy mercy on me, gracious Lord, do Thou bestow !

Ere yet the sun
Becometh blind
In all the sky
Where once it shined,
O lighten, Lord,
My darkened mind.
Thy mercy, O Thou gracious Lord, now let me find !

Before the trump,
Both loud and clear,
Proclaims to earth
Thine advent near,
Have pity, Lord,
O Saviour hear !
In mercy, O Thou gracious Lord, to me appear !

H. Burgess.
H. C. Leonard.

# ARABIA.

*FROM THE HYMYARITIC (ANCIENT ARABIC)*
(A.D. 400 [?]).

## LIX.—THE PASSAGE OF THE RED SEA.

By night the people enter the sea : the sea and the waves
    roaring.
The leader divideth the sea : its waves roaring.
Like a frightened horse, the people pass quickly over the
    sea bottom.
The enemy weeps for his dead, the virgins wailing.
The waters, let loose to reflow ; the sea pouring down over
    whelms them.
The people hasten, the tribes descend into the deep.
They enter the waters, they pass through the midst.
The people are filled with stupor and great astonishment,
Although the ETERNAL is their keeper and companion.

C. FORSTER.

# ARABIA.

*FROM THE ARABIC OF MOHAMMED*
(A.D. 611).

## LX.—The Creed of Islam.

In the name of God :
The Compassionate, the Merciful !
Praise be to God, the Lord of the Worlds !
The Compassionate, the Merciful !
The King of the Day of Judgement.
Thee do we worship.   Thee do we ask for help !
Lead us in the right way :
The way of those to whom Thou hast been gracious,
Not of those against whom Thou art angry,
Nor of those who are in error !

*(In the rhymed style of the original.)*

When the earth with quaking is shaking,
When off her burden she is breaking,
And man demands, ' What aileth her ?'
On that day her tidings she shall be unfolding,
Which then the Lord revealeth her.
On that day shall men come in throngs, their works
 showing ;
And who one grain of good hath done, shows it then ;
And who one grain of ill hath done, shows it then.

# TURKEY-IN-ASIA.

*FROM THE SUMIRIAN* (B.C. 670).

## LXI.—A Penitential Psalm.

O MY Lord, my transgression is great!
Many are my sins!
O my God, Thou knowest that I knew not, my sin is great,
    my transgressions many!
The transgressions that I committed I knew not.
The sin that I sinned I knew not.
The forbidden thing did I eat.
The forbidden place did I trespass upon.
My Lord in the wrath of His heart did trouble me.
God in the strength of His heart did punish me.
God in the strength of His heart hath overwhelmed me.
God, who knew that I knew not, hath overshadowed me.
I lay upon the ground, and no one took me by the hand.
I wept, and my palms no one took hold of.
I cried aloud!   There was no one that would hear me.
I was in darkness and trouble.   I lifted not myself up.
To my God I referred my distress ; my prayer I breathed.
How long, O my God, shall I suffer?
The sin that I have sinned, do Thou turn to blessedness!

The transgression I have committed, let the wind carry
    away !
My manifold affliction, do Thou destroy like a garment !
O my God, seven times seven are my transgressions :
My transgressions are ever before me !

                                  VARIOUS.

# TURKEY-IN-ASIA.

*FROM THE ACCADIAN* (B.C. 650).

## LXII.—THE CREATION.

HE constructed dwellings for the great gods.
He fixed up constellations with figures like animals.
He made the year.   Into four quarters He divided it.
Twelve months He established with their constellations.
For the days of the year He appointed festivals.
He made dwellings for the planets, for their rising and setting.
And that nothing should go amiss, nor their course be retarded,
He placed within them the dwellings of Bel and Ea.
He opened great gates on every side.
He made strong the portals on the left and on the right.
In the centre He placed luminaries ;
The moon He appointed to rule the night,
And to wander through the night until the dawn of day.
Every month without fail He made holy assembly days.
In the beginning of the month, at the rising of the night,
It shot forth its horns to illuminate the heavens.
On the seventh day He appointed a holy day,
And to cease from all business He commanded ;
Then arose the sun in the horizon of heaven, in glory.

F. TALBOT.

*FROM THE BABYLONIAN OF KING NABONIDUS* (B.C. 540).

### LXIII.—A PRAYER FOR BELSHAZZAR.

NABONIDUS, King of Babylon, the worshipper of the great
    gods am I.

O Lord of the gods, King of the gods of heaven and earth,

Even of the gods of gods who inhabit heaven, the great ones,

Joy cometh at Thy entrance ! May Thy lips establish bless-
    ings,

Even the blessings of the temples of Thy great divinity !

Set the fear of Thy great divinity in the hearts of my men,
    that they err not !

For Thy great divinity may their foundations remain firm
    like the heavens !

As for me, Nabonidus, King of Babylon,

Preserve me from sinning against Thy great divinity !

Grant me the gift of a life of long days !

In the heart of Belshazzar, my eldest son, the offspring of
    my heart,

Plant Thou reverence for Thy great divinity !

Never may he incline to sin ! With fulness of life may he
    be satisfied !

SIR H. RAWLINSON.

*FROM THE ARMENIAN OF ST. NERSES* (A.D. 1150).

### LXIV.—The Mother of God.

Mary, Mother of our Maker,
Daughter sprung from kingly David,
Bearing for us the New Adam,
Ancient Adam's race renewing.

God's true Mother we confess thee ;
Hail as God, the Child thou bearest ;
With the angel's words we greet thee,
Echoing his note of gladness.

Dwelling-place of Light, be gladsome ;
Temple, where the true Sun dwelleth ;
Throne of God, rejoice, that bearest
Him, the Word of the Almighty.

Home of Him that none may compass ;
Hostel, where the Sun finds resting ;
Dwelling of the Fire of Glory,
Where the Word finds fleshly clothing.

[ 132 ]

Seers of old in figures saw thee—
Noah's Ark, the true, the living ;
Tent of Abraham our father ;
Moses' Bush, which flames consumed not.

Ark of Covenant and Mercy ;
Lamp, where wondrous light is burning ;
Censer of the sweetest incense,
Where the fourfold spices mingle.

Rain that David saw descending ;
Solomon's Garden, fair with blossoms ;
Spikenard, of the Spirit's sweetness ;
Valley where the lily bloometh.

Great Isaiah's Virgin, bearing ;
And Ezekiel's fastened Portal ;
Bethlehem's glory, seen by Micah ;
Daniel's great Stone-bearing Mountain.

Lo, we pray thee, Life's own Mother,
From the stain of sin to cleanse us
By thy prayer to God our Maker—
Unto whom be praise and glory.

W. H. KENT.

# PERSIA.

*FROM THE ZEND OF ZOROASTER* (B.C. 550).

## LXV.—The Light of Light.

God is the light of light, the living Creator of all things.
Perfectly wise is He, the Holiest One, the Eternal.
Father of all that is true, and Giver of life immortal.
Self-derived His glory, and His are the power and the
    kingdom.

Ere the creation of day, and before the creation of angels,
The Holy Spirit of God, the Word, hath continuously spoken.
Garnered and treasured in Him are all that is perfect and
    holy :
He is the type of creation, the First-born Son of the
    Father.

Diligent sowing is better than offering prayers by the
    thousand.
Uncompassionateness is the worst disease of the spirit.
Three are the rules of life : in these are the essence of
    virtue,
See that in thought thou art pure, and pure in word, and in
    action !

The mind of the guileless man aspires to the life immortal.

God is the Saviour of all, of every one of His creatures.

Ever, to them that adore, He is Friend and Brother and
Father ;

His dwelling-place is the home, the glorious reward of the
faithful.

E. DE BUNSEN.

H. C. LEONARD.

# PERSIA.

*FROM THE ACHAEMENIAN (OLD PERSIAN) OF KING CYRUS* (B.C. 536).

## LXVI.—The Conquest of Babylon.

MERODACH (Bel), the great Lord, the Restorer of His
    people
Beheld with joy the deeds of His vicegerent (Cyrus),
Who was righteous in hand and in heart.

To His city of Babylon He summoned his march;
He bade him take the road to Babylon;
Like a friend and comrade, He marched at his side.

Without fighting or battle, He caused him to enter
    Babylon;
Nabonidus the king, who worshipped Him not,
He gave into his hand.

The God who, in His ministry, raises the dead to life,
Who benefits all men in difficulty, who pray,
Has graciously drawn nigh to him, and made strong his
    name.

I am Cyrus, the king of legions, the great king ;
I entered Babylon in peace ;
In the palace of the kings I enlarged my throne.

Merodach, the great Lord, cheered the heart of His servant ;
My vast armies He marshalled peacefully in the midst of
    Babylon ;
The sanctuaries of Babylon I established in peace.

For restoring the Temple of Merodach I prepared ;
He graciously drew nigh unto me, Cyrus the King. His
    worshipper,
And to Cambyses my son, the offspring of my heart.

In peace we restored its front in glory ;
All the kings brought their rich tribute,
Even of all lands from the Upper Sea to the Lower Sea.

I restored the gods who dwelt in the cities to their places ;
I enlarged for them seats that should be long-enduring ;
All their peoples I assembled, and I restored their lands.

May all the gods that I have restored to their strong places
Daily intercede for me before Bel and Nebo
That they would grant me length of days !

May they bless my projects with prosperity !
May they speak for me to Merodach my Lord,
For me, Cyrus the King, and for Cambyses my son !
SIR HENRY RAWLINSON.

# PERSIA.

## LXVII.—A Hymn to Ali.

Beside Thy glories, O most great,
Dim are the stars, and weak is fate !
Compared to Thy celestial light
The very sun is dark as night.
Thine edicts Destiny obeys.
The sun shows but Thy mental rays !

Thy merits form a boundless sea
That rolleth to eternity.
To heaven its mighty waves ascend.
O'er it the skies admiring bend :
And, when they view its waters clear,
The wells of Eden dark appear !

The treasures that the earth conceals,
The wealth that human toil reveals,
The jewels of the gloomy mine,
Those that on regal circlets shine :
Are idle toys, and worthless shows,
Compared with what Thy grace bestows !

Mysterious being !   None can tell
The attributes in Thee that dwell !
None can Thine essence comprehend,
To Thee should every mortal bend,
For 'tis by Thee that man is given
To know the high behests of heaven.

The ocean-floods round earth that roll,
And lave its shores from pole to pole,
Beside the eternal fountain's stream
A single drop, a bubble seem :
That fount's a drop,—beside the sea
Of grace and love we find in Thee !

ROYAL ASIATIC SOCIETY.

# INDIA.

*FROM THE SANSKRIT* (B.C. 1000).

## LXVIII.—THE TRUE GOD.

In the beginning rose the Golden Child,
The Lord of all that is, who reigns alone.
The earth He stablished, and the sky up-piled ;
Then to what God shall we our offering bring ?

He who gives strength, the Giver of all breath,
Whose bidding all the glorious gods obey ;
Whose shadow is eternal life—and death !
Then to what God shall we our offering bring ?

He who through all the waking world doth reign
By His great power—the one and only King,
Whose rule doth every man and beast restrain ;
Then to what God shall we our offering bring ?

He whose almightiness the rolling sea,
And snowclad mountains, rivers far away,
Alike proclaim ; whose arms these regions be ;
Then to what God shall we our offering bring ?

He by whose word the shining sky is bright,
And earth stands firm—who built the highest heaven,
Who, in the air, divided out the light ;
Then to what God shall we our offering bring ?

He by whose will the heavens and earth stand sure,
And, with an inward trembling, upward gaze ;
O'er which the rising sun shines bright and pure ;
Then to what God shall we our offering bring ?

Where'er the mighty waterclouds were rife,
Where'er they sowed the seed, and lit the fire—
Rose He !—of glorious gods the only life ;
Then to what God shall we our offering bring ?

He who above the waterclouds forth shone—
The thunderclouds that lit the sacrifice—
God above all gods He, and He alone ;
Then to what God shall we our offering bring ?

O may He not destroy us, whose decree
Created earth and heaven, the Righteous One,
Who also made the bright and mighty sea ;
Then to what God shall we our offering bring ?

F. MAX-MÜLLER.

H. C. LEONARD.

# INDIA.

*FROM THE PALI OF GAUTAMA, THE BUDDHA* (B.C. 590).

## LXIX.—Buddha's Last Words.

Looking for the Maker of this tabernacle,
I have run through a course of many births, not finding
    Him ;
And painful is birth again and again !
But now,
Maker of the tabernacle, Thou hast been seen !
Thou shalt not make up this tabernacle again !
All Thy rafters are broken !
Thy ridge-pole is sundered !
The mind, approaching the Eternal, has attained to the
    extinction of all desires.

F. Max-Müller.

# INDIA.

## LXX.—A Morning Hymn in the Caiva Temple, vv. 1-4

Hail! Being, Source to me of all life's joys! 'Tis dawn;
  upon Thy flower-like feet twin wreaths of blooms we lay
And worship, 'neath the beauteous smile of grace benign
  that from Thy sacred face beams on us. Civa-Lord,
Who dwell'st in Perun-Turrai girt with cool rice-fields,
  where mid the fertile soil the expanding lotus blooms!
Thou on whose lifted banner is the Bull! Master!
  Our mighty Lord! from off Thy couch in grace arise.

The sun has neared the eastern bound; darkness departs;
  dawn broadens out; and, like that sun, the tenderness
Of Thy blest face's flower uprising shines; and so,
  while bourgeons forth the fragrant flower of Thine eye's
    beam,
Round the king's dwelling fair hum myriad swarms of bees.
  See Civa-Lord, in Perun-Turrai's hallowed shrine who
    dwell'st,
Mountain of bliss, treasures of grace who com'st to yield!
  O surging Sea! from off Thy couch in grace arise!

[ 143 ]

The tender Kuyil's note is heard ; the cocks have crowed ;
    the little birds sing out ; loud sound the tuneful shells ;
Star-lights have paled ; day's lights upon the eastern hill
    are mustering.   In favouring love O show to us
Thy twin feet, anklet-decked, divinely bright ;
    Civa-Lord, in Perun-Turrai's hallowed shrine who
      dwell'st !
Thee all find hard to know ; easy to us, Thine own.
    Our mighty Lord, from off Thy couch in grace arise !

There stand the players on the sweet-voiced lute and lyre ;
    there those that utter praises with the Vedic chant ;
There those whose hands bear wreaths of flowers entwined ;
    there those that bend, that weep in ecstasy, that faint ;
There those that clasp above their heads adoring hands ;
    Civa-Lord, in Perun-Turrai's hallowed shrine who
      dwell'st ;
Me too make Thou Thine own, on me sweet grace bestow !
    Our mighty Lord, from off Thy couch in grace arise !

G. U. POPE.

# INDIA.

*FROM THE TELEGU OF VEMANA*
(12TH CENTURY, A.D.).

## LXXI.—Spiritual Worship.

To pray and serve yet not be pure—
In offering bowl to place good food—
To worship God,—while suns endure
  Will never turn to good !

Our sins grow ever from our deeds,
Nor owe their birth and death to place ;
'Tis better then to see our needs
  Than look to works for grace.

Though hypocrites should meditate,
And perfect keep the outward law,
They ne'er attain the holy state,
  But sink in hell's dark maw !

The sanctity that God counts right
Is not in sky, or deserts rude ;
'Tis not where holy streams invite,—
  Be pure,—thou viewest God !

10

God looks not on our race or dress,
But dwelleth closely with the soul.
And those who don strange garb would bless
    Their bellies with your dole.

The quickly-dying flesh to please
Most men will bear continual pain ;
They will not risk a moment's ease
    Eternal bliss to gain !

What fools the pilgrims are !   They think
That God may not be found at home !
'Tis exercise alone !   They sink
    In woe,—then back they come !

To feed the hungry and the poor
Is nobler deed than sacrifice !
What greater good can man procure
    Than save the poor from vice ?

Some mortify the flesh,—and take
The name of ' Saints,' yet cannot cleanse
Their hearts !   Will you destroy a snake
    By scraping his defence ?

The sacrifice that fools lift up
Is never perfect,—brings no profit !
The dog that tries to lift a cup
    Will damage it or drop it !

                              C. P. BROWN.

# INDIA.

*FROM THE CANARESE OF SHADAKSHARA* (A.D. 1450).

## LXXII.—A Prayer for Mercy.

WELL know I how to stumble, and to fall,
  Yet know not how to rise !  O pity me !
Well know I how to speak, but not to walk.
    Of such Thou art the Lord : I come to Thee !
    Sinful am I and helpless : save Thou me !

I have no piety, no heavenly lore,
  No spirit of self-sacrifice have I,—
To guide me in my way : O pity me !
Of such Thou art the Lord : I come to Thee !
  O lift me up and save me, or I die !

For I am sinking in the fleshly wave
  And struggling with my woes.  O pity me !
  They praise Thy mercy, so I come to Thee !
Let them not mocking say : ' He cannot save !'
  Hast Thou no pity, Lord?  O save Thou me !

O Lord, I am not brave, no warrior I,
  And Thou hast placed me in a suffering frame,
· And left me there.  No help have I but Thee !
  Thou who destroyest sin, Thy help I claim
Whose mercy's boundless as the moon-lit sea.

T. HAINES.

[ 147 ]

10—2

# INDIA.

*FROM THE HINDI OF NANUK* (A.D. 1500).

## LXXIII.—THE ONLY NAME.

THE true Name is GOD,
Without fear, without enmity,
The Being without death,
The Giver of Salvation.
Remember the primal Truth,
Truth which was before the world began,
Truth which is,
Truth which will remain.
How can truth be told?
How can falsehood be unravelled?
By following the will of God,
As by Him it is ordained.
There is one self-existent:
He Himself is the Creator.
There is one that continueth:
Another never was, and never will be.
Thou art in each thing, and in all places, O God!
Thou art the one self-existent Being.
My mind dwells upon One,

Him who gave the soul and the body.
Numerous Mohammeds have there been,
Multitudes of Bramahs, Vishnus, and Sivas,
Thousands of Seers and Prophets,
Tens of thousands of Saints and Holy Men :
But the Chief of Lords is the One Lord,
The true name of GOD.
His attributes without end, beyond reckoning,
Who can understand ?

# INDIA.

*FROM THE MALAYALAM.*

## LXXIV.—Morning Hymn to Kali.

Thou givest all joy, with pleasures dost crown
Who worshippest Thee, at Thy feet bowing down ;
$\qquad$ Praised be Thou !

Thou art, as it were, the key of the earth ;
The Mother of all, we owe Thee our birth ;
$\qquad$ Praised be Thou !

When hunger attacks, or the heat of mid-day,
Thou givest us food, fatigue flies away ;
$\qquad$ Praised be Thou !

Thou givest each day Thy blessings in heaps,
Removest alarms ; Thy love never sleeps ;
$\qquad$ Praised be Thou !

Each day, ere the light, I crave for Thy grace,
And offer this prayer before Thy sweet face ;
$\qquad$ Praised be Thou !

Who daily repeat it, who hear it each morn,
Shall never lack food, their barns shall have corn ;
$\qquad$ Praised be Thou !

$\qquad$ A. G. Gover

# INDIA.

## LXXV.—To a Sacred Cow.

WHAT a fine cow your predecessor was !
How well she supported us with her milk !
Will not you supply us in like manner ?
You are a god amongst us—
Do not let the sacred place go to ruin ;
Let one become a thousand ;
Let all be well ;
Let us have plenty of milk.

W. E. MASHILL.

# INDIA.

### LXXVI.—THE CREATOR.

GREAT in heaven is Singbonga (Sun-Spirit) :
· He has created heaven and earth—
None is greater than He !

As we kindle a light in the house
So has Singbonga set the sun in heaven,
To lighten the whole world.

Hungry am I, but Singbonga will give to me—
He who feeds the ants and the birds—
Why should he not give to me ?

Our dead are gone into that land ;
The body is still, the soul moves on ;
O father, O mother, whither hast thou gone ?

J. JELLINGHAUS.

# INDIA.

*FROM THE KHOND.*

## LXXVII.—A Sower's Prayer.

Thou, O Boora Pennu, created us to hunger !
Thou gavest us every seed ;
Thou commandedst us to plough with bullocks ;
Grant, then, the prayers we now offer !
Save us from the tiger and the snake ;
Save us from stumbling-blocks ;
Let the seed appear to be earth to the eating birds ;
Let it appear to be stones to the eating animals ;
Let the grain spring up suddenly, like a dry stream swollen
    in a night.
Let the earth yield to our plough-shares, as wax melts
    before hot iron.
Let the sun-burnt clods melt like hailstones.
Remember that the increase of our produce is the increase
    of Thy worship.

Macpherson.

# INDIA.

*FROM THE GUZERATI* (19TH CENTURY).

## LXXVIII.—A PARSEE CREED.

WE believe in only one God, and do not believe in any beside Him.

He created the heavens, the earth, and the angels.

He created the sun, the moon and the stars.

He created the fire and the water, and all things of the two worlds.

In that God we believe, Him we worship, Him we invoke, Him we adore.

Our God has no face, nor form, nor colour, nor shape, nor fixed place.

There is no other like Him ; He is Himself alone.

He is so glorious that we cannot praise or describe Him.

God's true Prophet, Zoroaster, brought this religion to us from God.

D. NAOROJI.

# INDIA.

*FROM THE BENGALI OF KRISHNA PAL* (A.D. 1801).

### LXXIX.—The Friend of Sinners.

O THOU, my soul, forget no more
The Friend who all thy misery bore ;
Let every idol be forgot,
But, O my soul, forget Him not.

Jesus for thee a body takes,
Thy guilt assumes, thy fetters breaks,
Discharging all thy dreadful debt ;
And canst thou e'er such love forget?

Renounce thy works and ways with grief,
And fly to this most sure relief ;
Nor Him forget who left His throne,
And for thy life gave up His own.

Infinite truth and mercy shine
In Him, and He Himself is thine :
And canst thou then, with sin beset,
Such charms, such matchless charms, forget?

Ah ! no : till life itself depart,
His name shall cheer and warm my heart ;
And, lisping this, from earth I'll rise,
And join the chorus of the skies.

Ah ! no : when all things else expire,
And perish in the general fire,
This name all others shall survive,
And through eternity shall live.

J. Marshman.

# RUSSIA-IN-ASIA.

*FROM THE MONGOLIAN.*

## LXXX.—A Wanderer's Song.

God, who doth care for me
 In the barren wilderness,
 On unknown hills, no less,
Will my companion be.

When I wander lonely and lost
 In the wind ; when I watch at night,
 Like a hungry wolf, and am white
And covered with hoar-frost ;

Yea, wheresoever I be,
 In the yellow desert sands,
 In mountains, or unknown lands,
Allah will care for me !

Chodzko.
H. W. Longfellow.

# CHINA.

*FROM THE KOU OUEN, OR OLD CHINESE, OF CONFUCIUS* (B.C. 500).

## LXXXI.—The Root of Virtue.

GOD is the Father of men, compassionate, tireless in blessing.
Ever He dwelleth with men, beholding their ways and their
  doings.
Always omniscient is He, and never can He be mistaken ;
Marking the doing of wrong with just and holy displeasure.

Three are the rules of life, and three are the spheres of our
  duty :
Honour thy Father and Mother, for this is the root of all
  virtue ;
Honour the Rulers of States, for they are the fathers of
  nations ;
Honour the God of Heaven, for He is the Father of all men.

Wouldst thou approach, O man, and know the life that is
  perfect ?
Treat thy neighbour thyself as thou wouldst wish to be treated.
He who is good loveth all, for all men are but his brothers.
Love one another, O men, for love is the chief of the virtues.

VARIOUS.

H. C. LEONARD.

[ 158 ]

# CHINA.

*FROM THE MIDDLE CHINESE OF SU TUNG-P'O* (A.D. 107C).

## LXXXII.—An Elegy on a Reformer.

HE rode on the dragon to the white cloud domain ;
He grasped with his hand the glory of the sky.
Robed with the effulgence of the stars,
The wind bore him delicately to the throne of God.

He swept away the chaff and husks of his generation ;
He roamed over the limits of the earth ;
He clothed all nature with his bright rays ;
His rivals panted after him in vain.

Dazed by the brilliancy of his light
He cursed Buddha ; he offended his prince ;
He was banished far away to the distant south ;
He passed the grave of Shun and wept over the daughters
of Yao.

The water-god went before him and stilled the waves ;
He drove out the fierce monster as if it were a lamb,
But above in heaven there was no music, and God was sad,
And summoned him to his place beside the throne.

H. A. GILES.

# CHINA.

*FROM THE MANCHU.*

## LXXXIII.—THE PRAISE OF BUDDHA.

SHOULD I Buddha's power and glory,—
  Earth's Protector,—all unfold,
Through more years would last my story
  Than the Ganges' sands of gold !
Him the fitting reverence showing
  For a moment's period brings
Ceaseless blessing, overflowing
  Unto all created things.


If thou seek great Buddha ever
  With a heart devoid of guile,
He the mists of sin will sever,
  All before thee bright shall smile !
Whoso into deed shall carry
  What his holy precept saith
Through all time alive shall tarry
  And be free from life and death !

[ 160 ]

If with cataract's voice the story
  I through million ages roar,
Yet of Buddha's power and glory
  I could ne'er the sum outpour.
Buddha, thou who best of any
  Know'st the truth of what I've told,
Spread the tale, through regions many
  As the Ganges' sands of gold.

G. BORROW.

# CHINA.

*FROM THE OUEN-TSCHANG, OR MODERN CHINESE*
(A.D. 1890).

## LXXXIV.—THE NEW HEART.

Alas! my heart is black,
  By Satan sore deceived,
Far from the upward track,
  God's judgement disbelieved.
From heaven, O Holy Spirit, come!
With Christ's Gospel my heart illume.

Alas! my heart defiled!
  Its lusts and crimes grow fast;
My sins on high are piled
  For sore reward at last.
From heaven, O Holy Spirit, fly!
My heart with Christ's blood purify.

Alas! my heart of woe,
  With sorrow sick to death!
Fearing sin's doom to know,
  I sigh with wounded breath.
From heaven, O Spirit blest, descend!
With Jesus' peace my grief to end.

[ 162 ]

Alas ! my strengthless heart
  Is slow to love God's way,
To hate the wrong, love right,
  While worldly thoughts bear sway !
From heaven, O Spirit, come !  Complete
My heart, with Christ's perfection sweet.

A. SOWERBY.

.

# THIBET.

*FROM THE THIBETAN.*

### LXXXV.—Victory over Birth and Death.

THE Victorious One spoke these verses ;
Hearken unto me while I tell them.
What I say is to dispel sleep and torpor,
And to bring gladness to the mind.
The All-wise, the Protector, the Mighty One,
The very Compassionate One—He who had
Finished with corporeal existence spoke this :

> Alas, the mutability of created things !
> All that is created is subject to decay ;
> All that is born must come to destruction.
> Happy they who are at rest !

As a river that is always running swiftly by and never
    returns—
Such are the days of man's life ; they depart and come
    back no more.
Joy is fleeting and mixed with pain ; it swiftly dis-
    appears—
Like figures traced on water with a wand.

As the waters of a brook,
So flow on, by day and night, the hours of man's life ;
It draws nearer and nearer to its end.
The end of all that is hoarded is to be spent ;
The end of all that is lifted up is to be cast down ;
The end of meeting is separation ; the end of life,
　　death.
As the end of life is death, and all die—
So likewise do virtue and vice bear fruits
Which follow after the dead.

They who do evil go to hell ;
They who are virtuous go to happiness ;
They who have observed the Right Way, and those
　　who are without sin, obtain Nirvana.

Give yourselves then to the unceasing joy of medita-
　　tion.
See the end of birth and age in the birth of diligence.
Overcome the habits of evil and you shall pass, a
　　conqueror, beyond birth and death.

# JAPAN.

## LXXXVI.—THE VOYAGE OF LIFE.

LIKE to the waving grass, as it floats in the breeze of the
    evening :
Like to the rippling light, as it fadeth away in the twilight :
Like to the full-sailed ship, as she hasteneth home to her
    harbour :
Such is the life of man, as it ever floweth and ebbeth !

Wise and foolish alike embark on the out-going vessel,
Bending their oars, as they row across the bottomless ocean ;
Lightly the sails are spread, to catch the wind of the
    autumn ;
Quickly they hasten to enter the lustrous clouds of the sunset.

Multitudes fill the graves, but ever to the believer
Cometh immortal youth, and blest is he in departing.
Blessed are they who know and love the precepts of Buddha,
Teaching the love of man, and the way to the homes of the
    perfect.

ANON.

H. C. LEONARD.

# JAPAN.

*FROM THE AINO.*

## LXXXVII.—NATURE WORSHIP.

To the Sea, which nourishes us—
To the Forest, which protects us—
We give our grateful thanks.
You are two mothers that nourish the same child :
Do not be angry with us if we leave one and go to the
other !

I. BIRD.

# AFRICA.

# EGYPT.

*FROM THE ANCIENT EGYPTIAN.*

(From the 'Book of the Dead,' B.C. 2000.)

## LXXXVIII.—THE ETERNAL ONE.

THAT which hath been am I, and that which is,
And that which is to come, and none can lift
The veil which covereth me from mortal sight.

The world around, we cannot comprehend,
For God who made it hath forbidden this !
That which we speak in secret, all is known
To Him who made our souls, and He is near,
And present to us when we seem alone !

Who then can bless Thee ?   Who can render thanks
For Thee or to Thee ?   With what reverence
To Thee, O Father, shall Thy creature come?
I cannot comprehend Thine hour, Thy time !
How shall I love Thee ?   Not as though from self
My being sprung, as though I were mine own,
But rather as Thine own, and only Thine !

That which I am art Thou, that which I do,
That which I say !   All things, O God, art Thou,
All that is made, and all that is not made.
Thou art the Mind that comprehendeth all,
Thou also art the God that doeth all,
Thou art the Father that createth all !
Of all material things the subtlest part
Is air : of air, the soul : of souls, the mind :
And, of the mind, the subtlest part is God !
That which is truth, through me, doth praise the Truth.
That which is good, through me, doth praise the Good
They who love God, who love their fellow-men,
Find grace with God.   The mortal body dies,
The soul lives on !   It passes through the gate ;
It makes a way, up through the darkest gloom,
Unto its Father, to enjoy His face.

Various.
H. C. Leonard.

# EGYPT.

*FROM THE COPTIC.*

## LXXXIX.—A Liturgical Hymn.

O Thou true Light which lightest every one
That comes into the world!   Through love to man
Thou camest.   All creation hath rejoiced
That Thou didst come.   For Adam Thou didst save
From the beguiling that had wrought his fall,
And Eve Thou savedst from the pains of death,
And unto us hast given the filial spirit.
With all Thine angel-hosts we praise, we bless Thee.


O Christ our God, True Light of Human Kind!
When Thou dost cause the morning hour to shine
Let thoughts of light abound within our hearts.
Let not dark passion overwhelm our souls.
With mind and strength, like David, we would praise,
Like him would call on Thee, and cry aloud,
Who said : ' Mine eyes anticipate the dawn
That I may meditate upon Thy word.'

[ 173 ]

Lord, in Thy tender mercy hear our voice !
Saviour of those who put their hope in Thee,
O Thou who wilt have all men to be saved,
Grant us to live, this day, apart from sin.
Guide and protect our steps throughout this day.
So may we be like David in our praise,
Who said : ‘ I laid me down in peace and slept ;
And I awaked, for Thou sustainedst me.’

THE MARQUIS OF BUTE.
H. C. LEONARD.

# ABYSSINIA.

## *FROM THE ETHIOPIC.*

### XC.—Prayer of African Jews.

Thou, O Lord, hearest in Heaven the worship of The
    saints,
Hear us also when we cry unto Thee in Thy heavenly
    temple.
O Lord, be not angry with us, nor suffer us to be destroyed.
Remember the covenant with our fathers, whom Thou
    didst re deem out of Egypt's bondage.
Forgive us our sins, and blot out our transgressions, which
    have separated us from Thee.
O God of our fathers, turn unto us and cause us to live.
O God of Abraham, turn unto us and cause us to live.
O God of Isaac, turn unto us and cause us to live.
O God of Jacob, turn unto us and cause us to live.
O Lord, lead us into the right way, and give peace unto
    Zion, and salvation to Jerusalem.

H. A. Stern.

# MOROCCO.

*FROM THE MOORISH-ARABIC OF THE LATE EMPEROR OF MOROCCO.*

## XCI.—A MORNING HYMN.

GLORY be to God alone!
The shades of night are fled away,
The ruddy dawn leads in the day,
And light once more to mortal eyes is shown.
Bow before the Eternal King,
To His praise loud anthems sing
For all the benefits bestowed
By Him, the one, the only God.

W. C. TAYLOR.

# FRENCH CONGO.

## *FROM THE CABINDA.*

### XCII.—The Creation and Fall.

ZAMBI PUNGO (Spirit-God) created the whole world.
In His hand He bears thunder and lightning.
All men were by Him created white, but, having sinned
    against Him, they became black.
There was a room full of beautiful things, but the door was
    closed.
A woman, tempted by a man, threw open the door ;
Then the black dust descended, and both became black.
She ran, screaming, to the river Congo.
Afterwards the sacred palm-tree closed up its crown.
Thick clouds gathered over heaven and earth.
From the crown of the palm-tree birds were let loose ;
Then the sun shone forth, and the clouds fled ;
Njambi (goddess of wealth) came back.
Ships, with white people, came again.

J. Bastian.

### XCIII.—The Creation and Fall.

Onjama (the God who beams forth) is the Highest Being.
It is He that created Heaven and Earth.
Six days He created, but on the seventh He created not.
A woman He created first, and afterwards man and animals.
The earth is vast, but Onjama is the Highest.
The clouds of Heaven are the outer parts of Onjama.
Everything that Onjama has made is good.
He governs all things, and marks the conduct of men.
If the smith understands his work, Onjama has taught him.
When the cock drinks water, Onjama points him to it.
So long as Onjama slays thee not, thou shalt not die.
Wilt thou speak with Onjama, tell it to the wind !
In former days Onjama was very near to men ;
A woman angered Him, and He withdrew into the highest
  heavens.
Then He listened not to them, and there was famine.
They confessed their wrong, and entreated Him to send a
  counsellor,
Whereupon He sent them Obosomtna and his wife Ntuabea.
By these He promised rain in its season,
And bade them, when the rainbow appeared, to remember
  Him.

J. Madek.

# BRITISH WEST AFRICA.

## FROM THE ASHANTI.

### XCIV.—THE CREATION AND FALL.

IN the beginning God created three white and three black
pairs of men.

He laid upon the earth a calabash and a sealed leaf, giving
them the choice between good and evil.

Then the blacks chose the calabash, and within it were
pieces of gold and iron, and other metals, of which
they knew not the use.

But the whites took the sealed leaf, and behold it told them
everything.

Then was God angry with the blacks, and they wandered
away from Him.

They worshipped the spirits of the rivers, and of the
mountains, and of the woods.

J. BOWDIK.

# BRITISH SOUTH AFRICA.

*FROM THE BECHUANA (BASSUTO).*

## XCV.—The Creation of Man.

Mo-rimo first created the black, and then the white men.
To the white men He showed favour.
He gave them white clothing, and many beautiful things,
But to the black men only cattle, and the assegai, and the
art of rain-making.

E. Casalis.

# BRITISH SOUTH AFRICA.

*FROM THE ZULU.*

## XCVI.—A Prayer to Ancestors.

O PEOPLE of our house !
I pray for prosperity.
I have sacrificed these bullocks of yours.
The food which you ask of me, you have first given me.
I pray for cattle that may fill this pen.
I pray for corn, that many people may come,
So that you may be glorified.
I ask for children,
So that your name may never come to an end.

CALLAWAY.

# BRITISH SOUTH AFRICA.

## FROM THE AMAKOSA (SOUTH CAFFRARIAN) OF SICANA.

### XCVII.—THE BUSH OF REFUGE.

HE who is our Mantle of comfort,
The Giver of life, ancient, on high,
He is the Creator of the Heavens
And of the ever-burning stars.
God is mighty in the Heavens
And whirls the stars around the sky.
We call on Him, in His dwelling-place,
That He may be our mighty Leader,
For He maketh the blind to see.
We adore Him as the only good,
For He alone is a sure defence ;
He alone is a trusty shield ;
He alone is our bush of refuge ;
Even He, the Giver of life on high,
And the Creator of the Heavens.

T. PRINGLE.

*FROM THE KHOI-KHOI (HOTTENTOT).*

## XCVIII.—THE FATHER OF FATHERS.

THOU, O Tsuigoa (Red Dawn),
Father of fathers,
Thou art our Father!

Let the thunder-cloud stream,
Let our flocks live, please,
Let us also live!

I am very weak indeed
From thirst and hunger;
O that I may eat the fruits of the field!

Art Thou not, then, our Father,
The Father of fathers,
Thou, O Tsuigoa?

O that we may praise Thee,
O that we may give Thee in return!
Father of fathers, O Lord, O Tsuigoa!

T. HAHN.

[ 183 ]

# MADAGASCAR.

*FROM THE MALAGASY OF RAMANISA*

(who suffered martyrdom, July, 1840).

## XCIX.—A Martyr's Hymn.

Loud to the Lord your voices raise,
Extol His name, exalt His praise;
Publish the wonders of His hand
O'er all the earth, in every land!

'Tell of the pity of the Lord,
Of grace and mercy!   Preach the word!
For wonderful to us appears
The love for us He ever bears.

Though guilty, we're with pardon crowned;
Condemned and lost, we now are found;
Though dead, new life to us is given,
And everlasting life in heaven!

O God, our God, to Thee we cry!
Jesus, the Saviour, be Thou nigh!
O sacred Spirit, hear our prayer,
And save the afflicted from despair!

Scarce can we find a place for rest
Save dens and caves, with hunger pressed;
Yet Thy compassion is our bliss,
Pilgrims amidst a wilderness.

# AMERICA.

# GREENLAND.

*FROM THE GREENLANDIC.*

## C.—A Dirge for a Drowned Son.

Woe is me that I see thy empty seat !
In vain has thy mother toiled to dry thy garments.
Behold, my joy is gone into darkness !
It has crept into the cavern of the mountain !
Once I went out at evening glad at heart ;
With straining eyes I watched for thy coming ;
Thou camest, most manfully rowing,
Emulously vying in the race with young and old.
Never didst thou return home empty !
Thus shall it never more be again !
My heart yearns when I think of thee !
Ah, my friends, could I weep as ye weep
Then would there be some solace for me,
But what have I now left to wish for ?
Death only can bring relief to me ;
I find my joy in rejecting what once I desired.

DALAGER.

# CANADA.

*FROM THE ESKIMO, OR INNUIT, OF JOHN AMOS.*

## CI.—A Hymn of Praise.

Praised be God,—
Who protecteth and feedeth this congregation,
Who subdueth the enemies of His people
And bringeth them to shame !
He beholdeth all their works ;
He chastiseth the disobedient
So that they may be brought to repentance ;
And because He Himself was tempted
He is able to succour the tempted.

# CANADA.

## CII.—A Dance Chant.

Hail! Hail! Hail!

Listen, O Creator, with an open ear to the words of Thy
people, as they ascend to Thy dwelling!

Give to the keepers of Thy faith wisdom rightly to do Thy
commands.

Give to our warriors, and to our mothers, strength to per-
form the sacred ceremonies appointed.

We thank Thee that Thou hast kept them pure unto this
day.

Listen to us still!

We thank Thee that Thou hast spared the lives of so many
of Thy children to take part in these exercises.

We thank Thee for the increase of the earth,

For the rivers and streams,

For the sun and moon,

For the winds that banish disease,

For the herbs and plants that cure the sick,

For all things that minister to good and to happiness.

We pray for a prosperous year to come.

Lastly we give Thee thanks, our Creator and Ruler !

In Thee are embodied all things !

We believe that Thou canst do no evil ;

We believe that Thou dost all things for our good, and for
our happiness.

Should Thy people disobey Thy commands, deal not
harshly with them !

Be kind to us, as Thou hast been to our fathers, in times
long gone by !

Hearken to our words as they ascend—

May they be pleasing to Thee, our Creator !

Preserver of all things visible and invisible.

E. S. PARKER.

# CANADA.

## CIII.—A Voyager's Prayer.

O Great Spirit,
Thou hast made this lake ;
Thou hast also created us as Thy children ;
Thou art able to make this water calm
Until we have safely passed over.

TANNER.

# UNITED STATES.

*FROM THE LENAPE.*

## CIV.—A National Hymn.

O POOR me,
Who now goes forth the enemy to meet,
And knows not if, with home-returning feet,
He shall come back, and wife and children greet !
    O poor creature,
Who cannot guide his life from day to day ;
    Who has no power his body to preserve ;
Who tries to do his duty as he may,
    The welfare of his native tribe to serve !
O Thou Great Spirit, dwelling in the skies,
    Take pity on my children and my wife ;
    Keep them from sorrowing for my threatened life ;
Give me success in this my enterprise.
O grant that I may kill my enemy,
    And win the trophies of victorious fight ;
    Have pity, and preserve me by Thy might,
And I will offer sacrifice to Thee !

M. Quatrefages.<br>H. C. Leonard.

[ 192 ]

*FROM THE OSAGES.*

## CV.—A RAIDER'S PRAYER.

O WOHKONDA (Master of Life) pity me !
I am very poor ;
Give me what I need ;
Give me success against my enemies :
May I be able to take scalps !
May I be able to take horses !

D. G. BRINTON.

# MEXICO.

*FROM THE AZTEC, OR NAHUATL* (14TH CENTURY).

## CVI.—A Warrior's Prayer.

O Lord, the Friend and Helper of men !
Invisible and impalpable Protector !
Lord of battles !   A war draws on ;
The god of war opens his mouth ;
Hungry is he ; he will drink the blood of the slain.
The sun and the god of the earth will rejoice ;
The gods of heaven and of the lower world will feast.
They look down upon those who shall conquer and upon
    those who shall die ;
The fathers and mothers of those who are to die know it
    not !
Grant, O Lord, that the fallen be graciously received by the
    sun and the earth,
The father and mother of all, in whose heart love dwells.
O Friend of men, we flee unto Thee !
May those who fall in battle be received in love and
    honour
Among the heroes who fell in former days !
There shall they enjoy unheard-of pleasures ;

They shall praise our Lord the sun in constant songs ;
They shall breathe the sweet perfume of the flowers ;
They shall intoxicate themselves with delights ;
They shall not number the days or the nights ;
Nor shall they reckon the years and the ages.
Their power and happiness shall be endless,
And the flowers whose perfume they breathe shall never
 fade.

J. AUSLAND.

# MEXICO.

## CVII.—A Psalm of the West.

God, in whose life is our life, O Thou who art everywhere
    present,
Thou to whom all things are known, Dispenser of all that is
    perfect,
Thou whom no eye can behold, Thou boundless perfection
    of goodness,
Under Thy wings is repose, and infinite shelter for ever!

Live thou in peace with all, and injuries suffer with meekness.
Leave thine avenging to God, unto Him who doth look
    upon all things.
Feed thou and clothe the poor, whatever thy cares and
    privations.
Truly their flesh is thy flesh : men are they even as thou art !

Like to the willow-trees green are the transient pomps of
    our life-time ;
They, if they live to be old, meet their end in the flame
    that devours them,

[ 196 ]

Else are they hewn by the axe, or upturned by the blast of
the tempest.

Saddened are we, and bowed down, by age and corruption
approaching ;

All things on earth pass away, predestined to fade and to
perish :

So, in the height of enjoyment, there cometh unpitying
weakness,

Suddenly seizing upon them, until in the dust they are
fallen.

All the round earth is a tomb, and of all that doth live on
its surface,

Naught is there born or upreared but what to the dust is
returning !

Glories of monarchs and victors all vanish to nothing
together,

E'en as the threatening smoke from the crater of Popoca-
teepell !

Earliest and latest of men alike in earth's bosom are
mingled !

Yet, let us stand, O friends, sustained by a confident
courage !

Let us aspire unto heaven, where all is unchanged and
eternal !

Everything there liveth on, and defieth approach of corruption.

Even the tomb, with its woe, is only the sun's lowly cradle.

And sorrowful shadows of death are but lights for the sky in
its glory.

M. CHEVALIER.<br>H. C. LEONARD.

# YUCATAN.

*FROM THE MAYA OF NAHAU PECH* (A.D. 1450).

## CVIII.—A WATCH-CRY.

WHAT time the sun shall brightly shine
   Tearful shall be the eyes of the king ;
Four ages yet shall be inscribed,
   Then shall come the holy priest, the holy God !
With grief I tell what now I see ;
   Watch well the road, ye dwellers in Itza !
The Master of the earth shall come to us !
     Thus prophesies Nahau Pech, the seer,
     In the days of the fourth age,
     At the time of its beginning.

D. G. BRINTON.

# GUATEMALA.

*FROM THE QUICHE.*

## CIX.—A PRIMITIVE PRAYER.

'THUS spoke from below those who saw the sun rise : for they all had but one language ; they did not as yet pray to either wood or stone ; they remembered only the word of the Creator and Fashioner, the Heart of Heaven and Heart of Earth ; and full of love, obedience, and fear, they offered their prayers, and, raising their eyes towards heaven, asked for daughters and sons, saying :

Hail, O Creator and Fashioner, Thou who seest and hearest !
Do not forsake us, O God, who dwellest in earth and in heaven.
Thou art the Heart of the earth, and Thou art the Heart of
    the heavens !
Long as the day shall dawn, O give to us sons and give
    daughters.
Let there be seed for the ground, and let there be light for
    our footsteps.
Lead us in open paths, and let not an ambush surprise us.
Let us ever be quiet, and live in peace with our dear ones.
Give to us joy in our days, and a life secure from reproaches.

ABBÉ DE BOURBOURG.<br>H. C. LEONARD.

# PERU.

*FROM THE KETSHUA* (13TH CENTURY).

## CX.—To the Rain Goddess.

Fair Princess,
Thine urn
Thy brother hath broken,
Even now, into fragments !
From the blow
Noise and fire, and
Lightnings proceeded !
Still, O Princess,
Thy moisture
Dispensing, thou rainest,
And all around
Thou makest it shower ;
And sometimes
Thou sendest forth snow.
For this labour
The Earth-builder—
The Creator of the earth—
Hath appointed thee
And hath made thee.

TSCHUDI.

# PERU.

*FROM THE TOLTEC.*

## CXI.—At an Inca Sacrifice.

O Inti, Lord of the sun,
Behold what thy children offer unto Thee !
Accept it, and be not wrath with them.
Grant unto them life and health,
And bless their fields.

J. G. Müller.

# PATAGONIA.

*FROM THE ARAUCANIAN.*

CXII.—A Prayer from the Far South.

O Father, Great Man,
King of this land !
Favour us, dear Friend, every day,
With good food,
With good water,
With good sleep.
Art Thou hungry ?
Poor am I, poor is this meal ;
Take of it, if Thou wilt.

A. Guinnard.

# OCEANIA.

# NEW ZEALAND.

*FROM THE MAORI.*

## CXIII.—A Farmer's Prayer.

My spirit trembles in the world,
  Whilst down from mountain heights
The lightnings flash, and winds descend !
    I offer sacrifice.
      O Io !


O God of men, my spirit yearns !
  Drive back my enemies,—
The earthquake, and the cataract,
  And all-devouring blight !
      O Io !


O God of men, regard my work !
  Behold, my crops I plant ;
O moisten my plantation soon,
  And cause my crops to grow !
      O Io !

O cloud, descend from mountain height,
   Ye lightnings flash and winds descend,
And grant an increase great,
   Whilst I my offering make,
And chant my sacred song,
   To Thee, the One Supreme !
     O Io !

J. WHITE.

# TASMANIA.

## FROM THE NARRINYERI.

## CXIV.—THE GIFT OF FIRE.

LONG ago our fathers lived all over the land.
They had no fire.
On the summit of the hill were seen two black men standing.
They threw down fire like a star.
It fell among the black men, my countrymen.
They were frightened; they all fled away.
They returned; they hastened; they made a fire with wood.
No more was fire lost in our land.
The two black men are in the clouds.
On a clear night you see them, like two stars shining.
These are they who brought fire to my land.

MILLIGAN.

# POLYNESIA.

## CXV.—A Dirge for a Child.

THE little voyager is ready to start !
Thy father is distracted for his boy !
The rocks re-echo the cries
Of thy heart-broken mother !

Should an ill wind overtake thee,
Seek shelter, O my spirit-child !
Go on thy way, fated voyager !
Go seek some other land,
Then return to fetch me !
'Tis a spirit-pilgrimage, O mother !

    Thy father is distracted for his boy !
    The rocks re-echo the cries
    Of thy heart-broken mother !

Speed thee on thy voyage to spirit-land,
Where a profusion of garlands awaits thee.
There the bread-fruit tree, pet son,
Is ever laden with fruit !
Yes, there the bread-fruit tree
Is for ever in season, my child !

Thy father is distracted for his boy !
The rocks re-echo the cries
Of thy heart-broken mother !

Awake, thou spirit-bearing vessel !
Gently waft him over the ocean !
Yonder is a frail bark !
'Tis a canoe full of spirits from Mangaia,
Hurried over the sea by fierce currents !

Thy father is distracted for his boy !
The rocks re-echo the cries
Of thy heart-broken mother !

O for a shelter from the tempest
On some well-sheltered shore !
Yes, on some well-sheltered shore !
The mourners mourn for the dead,
But thou, and thy sister, have reached
The gathering-place of spirits,
Whilst we lament.

Thy father is distracted for his boy !
The rocks re-echo the cries
Of thy heart-broken mother !

Prosperous be thy perilous voyage !
May soft zephyrs waft thee on !
Maybe thou hast miscarried,—
Too late to accompany the spirits
Which are hurried o'er the sea by fierce currents ?

Thy father is distracted for his boy !
The rocks re-echo the cries
Of thy heart-broken mother !

W. GILL.

14

# POLYNESIA.

## *FROM THE SAMOAN.*

### CXVI.—A Family Prayer.

O GODS, here is ava for you to drink !
Look kindly towards this family ;
Let it prosper and increase ;
Let us all be kept in health ;
Let our soil be productive ;
Let food grow abundantly for us, your creatures.
O war gods, here is ava for you !
Let there be a mighty people for you in this land.
O sailing gods, do not come on shore at this place ;
Be pleased to depart on the ocean to some other land.

TURNER.

# POLYNESIA.

*FROM THE PAPUAN.*

## CXVII.—A Sacrificial Prayer.

Compassionate Father!
There is some food for Thee,—
Eat it, and be kind to us on account of it.

.

# POLYNESIA.

*FROM THE MELANESIAN.*

## CXVIII.—A Prayer at Sea.

O Qat and Marawa,
Cover with your hands the blow-hole from me,
   that I may come into a quiet landing-place.
Let it calm well down away from me.
Let the canoe, which is yours and mine,
   go up into a quiet landing-place.
Look down upon me !
Prepare the sea, which is yours and mine,
   that I may go upon a safe sea.
Beat down the crest of the waves from me.
Let the breakers sink down away from me.
Beat them down level, that they may go down and roll away.
   that I may come into a quiet landing-place.
Let the canoe, which is yours and mine,
   turn into a whale, a flying fish, an eagle !
Let it leap on end over the waves.
Let it pass over to my land.

R. H. Codrington.

# POLYNESIA.

*FROM THE RAROTONGAN\* (circa A.D. 1800).*

## CXIX.—A Prophecy of Change.

O sons beloved,
Tread gently !
Rush not into evil,
Or into deadly war !

O sons beloved,
Tread gently !
For seasons bright
Of shining light,
As full-moon night,
Shall yet be seen !

O may you live,
My sons beloved,
To see the day
When good prevails,
And joy abounds !
The present lasts not !

\* The island of Rarotonga was discovered about 1820.

# POLYNESIA.

## *FROM THE FIJI* (A.D. 1850).

### CXX.—CHRIST RISEN.

THE Saviour of mankind has expired,
And the gloom of an eclipse covers the world;
The Sun is ashamed, and ashamed is the Moon!

The world's atonement buried lies;
Three nights it lay in the grave,
And the inhabitants of Judæa rejoiced!

Then of the angels there came two;
The faces of these two flamed like fire,
And the children of war fell down as dead!

They two opened the sepulchre of stone,
And the Redeemer rose again from death;
The linen lay folded in its place!

I stamp underfoot the tooth of the grave!
Where now, O death, is thy might?
Take to thyself thine envenomed sting!

I pledge a wide-spread salvation!
Shout triumphantly, sons of the earth,
For feeble now is the tooth of the law!

T. WILLIAMS.

# INDEX OF AUTHORS AND TRANSLATORS.

*[Original authors are distinguished by italics.]*

# INDEX OF SUBJECTS.

# INDEX OF FIRST LINES.

THE END.

*Elliot Stock, 62, Paternoster Row, London, E.C.*

# OTHER WORKS by THE LATE HENRY C. LEONARD.

## THE GOOD NEWS AFTER MARCUS' TELLING.

A literal translation of the Anglo-Saxon version of St. Mark's Gospel. With Preface and Notes. Second and Improved Edition. Price 1s.

'The unversed in Early English will thank Mr. Leonard for this little book. The translation reads well, and there are many passages that for vigour compare favourably with more modern versions.'—*Church Times.*

'This charming little book gives a new and delicate freshness and savour to the ancient Gospel of St. Mark. No one should fail to procure it It is singularly beautiful and suggestive.'—*Christian World.*

'A little work having peculiar charms. It gives the reader a good idea of the Bible as read by our ancestors during a period of nearly five centuries.'—*Christian.*

'A highly interesting document, and we are greatly obliged to Mr. Leonard for putting it within the reach of those to whom the English tongue of twelve centuries ago is unintelligible.'—*Westminster Gazette.*

## SONNETS ON THE PARABLES OF OUR LORD.

With a new classification and a new nomenclature; to which are added short poems on the Themes of Great Pictures. Dedicated by permission to the late Archbishop Trench. Second Edition. Cloth, price 2s.

'An interesting work which appeals to Christians of all denominations. The poems are graceful compositions, calculated to enhance the reputation of the author.'—*Christian World.*

'These Sonnets display poetic power of no mean order. The book is valuable not only from a literary, but from a theological standpoint, and forms a suggestive and helpful contribution to the discussion of an important part of our Lord's teaching. The classification is at once natural, logically consistent, and ingenious, and will prove of material assistance to the Bible student.'—*Freeman.*

## JOHN THE BAPTIST. An Epic Poem in

Three Books.   Cloth, 8vo., price 1s. 6d.

'Mr. Leonard has portrayed with rare skill and fidelity the genius and mission of our Lord's Forerunner.  His sketches of the social and religious life of the Jews, and of the marvellous scenes in which John was the most prominent figure, are powerfully drawn.   His language is simple, natural, and effective—the fitting vehicle for clear, fresh thought, suffused by deep and tender feeling, and enriched by the play of a chastened imagination.   That Mr. Leonard has the eye and heart of a poet is very evident.'—*Baptist Magazine.*

'We venture to give to this poem the strongest praise that so short a one on so well-worn a subject can receive.   Mr. Leonard has thought upon the character and work of John the Baptist until it has fired his soul, and then has poured it forth in graceful strains.'—*Sword and Trowel.*

## HALF-HOURS WITH THE APOSTOLIC

FATHERS.   Being a report of conversations which the Pilgrim had with Prudence, Piety, and Charity, in the Palace Beautiful, concerning the immediate disciples of the Apostles.   With Appendices on the Sacraments, Church Government, and Doctrine of the sub-Apostolic age.   Cloth, 8vo., price 1s. 6d.

## THE SPANISH ARMADA. A Ballad of Old

England.   Lord Macaulay's " Fragment " completed by another hand.   Price 6d.